The Man
Who Tried Out
for Tarzan

THE MAN WHO TRIED OUT FOR TARZAN

Stories by
HARRY H. TAYLOR

Louisiana State University Press
BATON ROUGE 1973

For Barbara

ISBN 0–8071–0061–7
Library of Congress Catalog Card Number 73–83911
Copyright © 1973 by Harry H. Taylor
All rights reserved
Manufactured in the United States of America
Set by The Colonial Press Inc., Clinton, Massachusetts
Printed and bound by LithoCrafters, Inc., Ann Arbor, Michigan
Designed by Dwight Agner

ACKNOWLEDGMENTS

"The Man Who Tried Out for Tarzan" first appeared in
Pyramid; "Tristan" in Prism International; "The Woman in
the Tree" in Quartet; "Carolyn" in Epoch; "The Diary of a
Short Visit" in Quest; "The Cage" in South Dakota Review;
and "The Madame Bovary Complex" in Western Humanities Review.

Contents

The Man
Who Tried Out
for Tarzan

Artemis and the Jogger

How can I invest with dignity and some importance a middle-aged man's interest in girls—not one girl, either, but many, thousands, so that in going to and from his classes Senton kept thinking that something should be done about this? Teaching has its occupational hazard: just the numbers, the steady stream, the crazy flow, as if some fundamental law having to do with the life force were being expressed, a law which nobody else seemed to notice.

When Senton came home from work he usually walked into an empty house. While he made himself a drink he considered the cat's claw marks in the curtains, the *Mad* magazines scattered across the floor, and the neatly stacked garbage which was waiting for him against the kitchen wall. However, this kind of loneliness is intangible and oblique, characterized by a certain unacknowledged numbness. He moved around these images for years without thinking much about them, one way or another, but things finally came to a head.

Senton wasn't terribly new in the block, but he still didn't know his neighbors, and when he walked the dog late at night he liked to peer into the houses as he passed. He was in an older, well-established, upper middle-class subdivision where the solidarity of people's lives was a comfort, a balm for the senses; and it soothed him to find behind slightly parted drapes rows of books, silver on the tables, and good prints.

Senton slowly passed a white brick Regency, a place that was as sterile, as clean-looking and as impregnable as a well-ordered fortress. Lights were on downstairs; and back behind the shrubbery, in a three-car garage that resembled a nineteenth-century stable, the door was up, a car gone; another light was burning in this empty, shell-like space. The front door opened. A tall girl in a skimpy bathing suit stood in the entrance for a moment looking at him. Embarrassed, Senton kept going, but the lateness of the hour, the heavy trees, the long shadows under the streetlamps, the muggy summer air, and the light coming from behind the girl within the huge house all worked on his imagination.

When Senton came home he wanted a drink. The house was empty, the kitchen upset. There were some martinis left in the pitcher from the night before, but he couldn't find a clean glass. He opened one cabinet after another searching for something to use, and finally, among the paper party napkins and the children's cereals, he

ARTEMIS AND THE JOGGER

found several Snoopy birthday cups. He poured a paper cup half-full, added ice, and sat down at the kitchen table.

Senton's wife came in. She threw the car keys on the table, filled a cup, and lit a cigarette. "The Arnolds aren't coming, the Fishers are out of town. The Hollanders, the Homesteads, and the O'Donnels don't answer their phones. So what am I supposed to do next? Whom do you suggest that I dig up?"

She was planning a home Communion. She was a liberal Methodist, but she was bringing in a young Roman priest who was much in demand among the ecumenical-minded crowd who sat on the floor in a circle, and while they passed the bread around, they publicly examined their consciences. When these middle-aged, middle-class people got going, they created the high-strung, slightly ragged intensity of a good sensitivity session.

Senton was still thinking about that tall thin girl, about that and about the clutter around him which reminded him of a crazy house. He shook the ice in his Snoopy paper cup and after a minute he tipped his head back, slowly chewing some of it. "I want a divorce," he said, chewing thoughtfully, "and I don't care how I get it. I don't care what you try to do or what it costs."

She looked at him without blinking. She didn't even ask him to repeat himself. She took the cigarette out of her mouth and tapped it lightly on the rim of the glass ashtray on the table. "I'm going to stay calm," she said, "but I'm also going to get to the bottom of this. You're having an affair, you're getting into one of your students."

Senton shook his head. He started to say something but

changed his mind. He knew that she wanted a scene, and that if she got it she could gradually wear him down. She looked like she was going to stay calm, but she finally picked up the ashtray and threw it against the wall, just missing his head. He picked up the car keys. He got to the front door before she could reach it, but when he was outside, on the porch, he had to hold the door against her, and as long as he was holding it he couldn't reach his car. He knew that if he did make it to the car she would hold onto the door handle, and if he tried to drive off he would have to drag her along, down the drive. Senton gave up, but when he came back into the house he wasn't the same man.

Senton thought of himself as a camera recording impressions, a delicate, temperamental machine. He maneuvered the mechanism here and there, working on long shots, close-ups, fancy angles, tricky techniques. He found himself working in the same places, wheeling the expensive equipment around.

The dormitory complexes rose above everything else. In their lobbies and huge lounges, spiraling free-form stairs appeared to float like massive metal sculpture overhead. The soft indirect lighting emphasized certain surfaces but cast others into shadow. The featureless music never stopped.

The bulletin boards were covered with new and outdated announcements, schedules of meetings, social events, services, notes on this or that: Ox Roast. Volleyball

Turnout. I.A.S.T. Meets. Alpha Mu Gamma Night. Dad's Day. Bicycle Race. Social Commitment Week. Trade Parties. Open House. MSU SWIM. Slave Auction Block. MGB (Cheap). Sigma Pi Car Wash. Plain Pill Talk. Student Charter Flight. Fish Fry. Frosh Fest. Circus Feed. S.O.S. Delta Sigma Pi Winter Rush.

THIS IS YOUR LIFE
WHAT ARE YOU GOING TO DO WITH IT?
Will you give it as much consideration as you do your money?
WHERE ARE YOU GOING?
WHY ARE YOU HERE?
The Church of Latter Day Saints is sponsoring an open house to answer these questions and many more like them concerning man's purpose here on earth. Refreshments! Free! Informal!

The dormitory activity was ceaseless, a perpetual coming and going among the curved couches, the big soft-bottomed chairs, the glass coffee tables, and the color TV sets. The girls got up to go out: brief jersey dresses, unbelievably brief, big-belted skirts, nifty bell-bottoms, sharp pants that hugged the hips, cut-down denims which emphasized with such frank joy the cute crotch.

Senton, of course, was a joyful mess. What could be done about this crazy flux, energy without direction or limit, part of the expanding universe? What could be done? Nothing. Right? *Nothing.* He finally felt depleted, depressed.

Senton stood on his front walk in his new jogging outfit. He was going to get back into shape, do something brisk, masculine, and at the same time lose some weight. He had never been out this early without a car. He felt light, fluttery. The winter sky was dismal, still half-dark, and he didn't like the quiet, either. He stretched, breathing in the early morning damp. He touched his toes several times to warm up. He anxiously glanced toward the neighbors' windows. Was he really going all the way? Getting out there to jog? Hippity-hop past the upper middle-class in these funny clothes? He casually strolled down the walk, getting ready to stick one foot into the street, and when windows didn't go up, doors suddenly fly open, he wondered if, after all, there was going to be anything to this. Live, let live.

He stepped into the street. Some birds, some winter starlings, swooped, circling around and around his head, setting up a terrible racket. He flapped his arms, hopping from foot to foot, ready to go back, but the birds finally disappeared. He stood there in the street for a moment trying to get his breath. Then, when he realized that everything next door was still quiet, he broke into a lumpy trot, his elbows out, his wrists up against his sides, his fingers closed into small, soft fists. He was going to make it.

The big rust-colored collie stood barking, showing his teeth, his tail lowered between his legs. The dog was just on the edge of his own property, as if he knew the precise limits of his territory and was going to kill Senton if he attempted to step over onto it.

Senton crossed to the other side of the street. "Who's

ARTEMIS AND THE JOGGER

trespassing? I'm not trespassing. I'm staying over here," he said, picking up speed.

The collie continued to bark, alerting the other dogs along the route.

A mean-looking little spaniel came out to investigate. This time the dog came into the street after the jogger, yapping around his heels and upsetting his stride.

Senton picked up a short stick. "If you nip me, you're going to get it, right between the eyes."

The spaniel dutifully followed him, nipping close to his heels while at the same time avoiding the stick. The dog acted as if it were a routine pursuit, a time-worn specialty, and when he saw another dog he turned Senton over to the newcomer. He hurried back to his own place without looking behind him.

They have names like Carolyn, Tina, Pam, Carole, Vicki, Cindy, Judy, Linda, Karen, Sharon, Gail, Candy, Jan, Sherry, Sandra, Cheryl—names like Donna, Debra, Dot. Their hair spreads across their backs, just below the shoulderblades. They have narrow little legs in white boots, bare, cold-looking little knees and half-bare, slightly plumpish thighs. They're small-town, middle-class girls, for the most part, but they dress in expensive boots, buckskin, cowhide. When they aren't in class, they're always talking. When they're alone with each other they use last names: Sloan, Smith, Small. They call each other "guys." They say: "Hey! Where did you guys go last night?" They stand with their books against their breasts, the slightly tilted pelvis curving the hip-line, and while they're talking their hair falls to one side. Senton loves the mouths—the healthy, brilliant, white, straight middle-class teeth.

Cheryl Berryman, Senton's student secretary, was slim and tall. She wore tank tops and cords, accentuating her little breasts, her narrow waist and her small, hard, slightly curved bottom. She had long, straight pale blonde hair, and when she had hung her coat in his office closet, she gave her hair a few hasty licks while standing there talking to him, her comb in her hand.

Senton was never sure just how innocent she was; he never knew what she knew and didn't know, but she was gradually taking over his office closet. She was a physical education major, and since she had to make quick changes between classes, she stored her gear in his closet: sweat shirts, sneakers, shorts, a tennis racket, and a battered pair of golf clubs.

The gym had dressing rooms and lockers. She *showered* in the gym, didn't she? While she used his closet, while she took advantage of the mirror on the closet door, she was gradually establishing a tenuous, quirky sort of relationship between them, and while he never actually caught her changing in there, she was creating a casualness that could be used if he wanted to use it.

Senton didn't know if he was supposed to worship at the shrine or jump her in the dark. Was he supposed to start an affair? Move in carefully. Discuss the spiritual life, loneliness, art, books, the great ideas. Kiss her first on the cheek, close to the ear. For the first six months, forget the breasts . . .

Cheryl specialized in running and jumping. When she was working for a friend of Senton's, an instructor in a large office filled with other instructors, he used to ask her how far she could jump from a standing position. She finally showed him. She drew a chalk line on the floor and jumped. How far would that be? She had shown his friend, but she had never shown him. The subject had never come up.

"I'm really run down this year," she said. "Do you feel run down? Did you think the winter was ever going to end? I thought the winter was never going to end. You know what I need, don't you? I need to get to Florida and bake, but I don't know . . ."

Senton often consulted her about his jogging, getting advice about distance and stress situations. "I finally struck up a deal with those dogs," he said. "I stock up on cheap cold cuts, and when I see a dog I pitch the cold cuts as far as I can, sometimes into yards, sometimes up trees, sometimes on front porches, and while they're killing themselves over the spoils, I calmly pass on, getting in some serious jogging, some pretty professional stuff."

Cheryl put her comb back in her purse. "*Cold cuts? Every day?* Doesn't that get pretty expensive?"

"You should see what it's doing for my pitching arm."

"Pitching arm?"

"Man is resourceful. A creature who uses his head. What does the universe know?" he said.

11

"When I was in Florida last year—over the spring vacation?—you couldn't *move* on the beaches. You couldn't *move*, there were so many people, and—honestly—you couldn't separate other people's limbs from your own. Do you think I'm kidding? I'm not kidding. The crowds! The boys picked up this foreign custom, and when they met you they didn't shake your *hand*, or anything like that. Do you know what they did? They pinched your bottom. *Everybody* did it, it's just done. Can you imagine? God! Did I never get sore . . . I wore this fairly conservative, two-piece job at first because I'm pretty modest, I really am, but I finally felt silly being so covered up. So I finally bought this *terribly* expensive, *terribly* skimpy thing. It cost enough. It cost a fortune. You wouldn't believe it. I mean, a little while back they'd bust you for wearing something like that. God. I liked it, though, I really did. You know? But at the same time, if you want to know the truth, if you want to know the real truth, I never really felt comfortable in it, when I was *practically bare*, when there was nothing there, really, but just *me* . . ."

Senton paused in the middle of the street. The late March air had a moist spring smell. In the mist, in the early morning wet, there was a sort of odd oriental effect; the bare, dripping trees looked as if they had been etched; and, for a moment, he considered the world to be a very mysterious place. He felt vaguely excited, as if he might be onto something pretty big. He broke into a good trot.

A chow came out to the edge of the lawn and stood

ARTEMIS AND THE JOGGER

there on sturdy legs, barking, showing his teeth. Spittle ran down the sides of his mouth.

"You must be new on this beat," the jogger said, "if you don't know about the goodies."

The chow hesitated for a moment. Senton sailed the baloney through the air. The dog ran yipping across the yard after it.

The light was generally tricky, unsafe. The milk truck almost ran him down once, and, in the same morning, while he was coming back, the truck, coming back, got a second chance. The houses usually stayed dark. Senton felt completely separated from the lives going on in the big houses, a furtive shadow dodging dogs and milk trucks.

Slave for a Day
Try Us

Lambda Chi Alpha advertised in the school papers and in the local press. Enterprising middle-class Americans who knew how the system worked. Girls filled with interesting juices. Girls going up. A boisterous little harem with its eye on the buck. Some good clean fun. Some promising, some playing around, some backing up. They knew what the score was, and while they offered the standard services like baby-sitting, housecleaning, and some mild yard work, they were also into a few novelty items like a good back rub.

They had taken over a filling station a few blocks from the campus, and when Senton drove in for gas they crowded around the car holding up their car-wash signs.

They waved the signs around in front of his windshield, putting on the heat. Small, shyish, delicate, vaguely curved little girls in among the bigger, meaty types. Battered jeans and bare feet. Tye-dye shirts carelessly knotted around the middle, just above the navel.

Senton drove around to the side of the station where they were waiting with the hose. He sat behind the streaming windows, and while they dragged sopping sponges across the hood, he lit a cigarette. They moved around the car, stretching up on their toes to reach the top, but, like women, they stood away from the job instead of leaning into it. They wiped their foreheads with the backs of their arms, their shirts clinging to their spines or around their breasts in damp spots. They talked to each other while they worked, without looking inside the car, as if he weren't sitting there.

Cheryl Berryman was working on his wheels, sloshing a huge, hard brush into a bucket and then trailing the sudsy water across the tires. She was wearing a simple, stretchy, one-piece swimsuit, and her long blonde hair, parted in the middle, was tied behind her head. She picked up her bucket, and while she was getting up off her knees, she suddenly recognized him. She briefly waved, but she moved on without speaking. Senton watched her disappear in his rear-view mirror. He put out his cigarette.

The line was growing. The cars were coming in from the street in a steady progression. The girls were already turning the hose onto the car behind him. They shook his car slightly while drying it, a subtle, swaying motion which

ARTEMIS AND THE JOGGER

aroused him, but they were suddenly through. They stepped back.

"Okay. That's it. You're done."

He started the car. He moved out slowly, around the crowds, but when he stopped to pay them at the end of the line, Cheryl was waiting for him.

She was wearing jeans again. She was buttoning her shirt on over her swimsuit. "Where're you going? I've got to get back to the dorm. I'm *sopping* under these clothes. Will I hurt the car? Hey! Wait a minute," she said, starting to climb in, "I promised to meet somebody here. I'll catch hell if I don't stick around. I'm a slave these days in more ways than one."

Senton was setting the alarm earlier and earlier, and he slept fitfully. When he rose he spent fifteen minutes on a bicycle exerciser, building up his circulation before he actually went out. He was running farther and farther these days, getting into a part of the development that he had never noticed before. It was older, cheaper, less kept up. The small, square prefabricated houses couldn't have been over the ten- or twelve-thousand-dollar bracket. Carports replaced garages and then the carports stopped. There were chain link fences, bird baths, plastic flamingos, rock grottos with indiscriminate saints. The dogs here were usually strays. They traveled together in packs. They had a wild, hungry, lonely look, and when he threw the cold cuts they fought among themselves over every last scrap.

Senton's wife woke. She didn't have her eyes entirely

open yet. She fumbled around the bedside table until she found a cigarette. She lit the cigarette and lay back on the pillows watching him on the exerciser with her arm flung across her forehead. She had a mild coughing fit, and when it passed her eyes looked wet.

She still didn't believe that Senton merely ran around the neighborhood, at least not without climbing into windows and rolling around in strange beds. "Some day," she said, "I'm going to get to the bottom of this. I'm going to find out just where you actually go."

Senton didn't stop pedaling. He didn't answer her.

Joyce scratched the back of her head and then looked at her nails. "Senton," she said, "I'm trying to understand you; I'm trying to deal with this; I'm trying to come to terms with whatever I have to come to terms with; maybe you think you're the Man from Glad or something, but I *really* don't understand why you have to run around all over the universe on Sunday morning, too."

Senton wasn't actually sure about the calendar anymore. "I don't want to miss a day. You don't know how fast a man can deteriorate," he said.

In the Middle Ages the early guilds pulled gaudy allegorical representations of the seasons on lumbering platforms; the good burghers poured out to see the village girls going by as the nude graces. Here in the middle of America there is a brief period toward the end of the spring term, just before final examinations, when these girls, as if given a tribal signal, parade around the campus in as little as possible. Hundreds, thousands. They're everywhere. They're even

ARTEMIS AND THE JOGGER

overhead. They unexpectedly turn up on dorm roofs, precarious peaks, high places, oiling down, and even on windy, hazy days, they're up there busy turning brown.

Senton gingerly walked around the crowds on his way to his office—girls lying on their stomachs on the grass with their chins in their hands, their weight on their elbows, their little rumps up. Girls dotted here and there among the trees in various mythic lights, as if some of these girls might also be trees. Girls hurrying to classes, cutting through the library, coming out of the Student Union carrying Cokes in paper cups, their heads lowered, and while they're pulling the Cokes up through the plastic straws, they are wearing dreamy, removed expressions. Girls sitting on the steps, leaning against the railing, shove over a little to let Senton through, but he still has to squeeze past—their bare knees raised, their legs pressed together, held slightly sideways. Senton took the elevator up to his office.

Cheryl Berryman was standing in his office closet pulling on her jeans, obviously trying to get her jeans on before he could get into the office, and while she was wearing a top, she was hopping around on one foot having trouble with her pants. The battered golf bag filled with clubs suddenly dropped out of the closet, just missing his feet. He stepped back into the hall, slamming the door at the same time— as if the golf clubs were after him.

The warmish dark felt rainy. The spreading dawn stayed menacing, a cold glow, like something burning in an abandoned lot on the other side of the development.

Senton was getting into his jogging clothes. "I'm late this morning."

Joyce briefly raised her head. "*I'm* not going to ask any more questions," she said.

The drizzle was still coming down. The dogs were out together, chasing a cat. The cat dashed up a tree, and, in the swaying middle branches, trying to keep its balance, it stood there spitting, arching its back.

The dogs gave up. They turned on Senton.

He gripped the damp bag, and, at the last moment, just before a small beagle with one eye reached his ankles, he threw a fistful of cold cuts across the street.

Then the needlelike drizzle settled in, picking up strength. The rain, still very fine, began to pelt him with personal attention. He was getting soaked, but he wouldn't stop, and as he ran, his feet squishing in his tennis shoes, he tried to keep the damp paper bag close to his body.

The mist rolled in. He saw a car coming around the bend, but he could only vaguely make out the blurred headlights. He stepped back to let it pass, a big station wagon like his. Was it his? He couldn't be sure. He paused for a moment. Then he remembered that he was supposed to be jogging, and he got on the road again.

The dogs came up from behind. He wheeled around to throw the meat, but he stumbled at the same time, and as he went down he dropped the bag. He picked up the bag, just ahead of the dogs, but the sopping paper fell apart, and while the dogs leaped on the last of his supplies, he ran on, getting out of there as fast as he could.

ARTEMIS AND THE JOGGER

He was soon in a maze of short crisscrossing streets and dead-end lanes. He finally realized that he had left the development itself, and he wasn't sure now just where he was. The sidewalks abruptly ended, the streets were filled with chuckholes. There was a dense, almost unpleasant sweetness in the air, as if summer had begun earlier here. A heavy, dark vine on a trellis leaned backwards against the weather. The huge, dim, dilapidated Victorian houses were farther and farther apart. Broken porch swings rattled on their chains, tires dangled, swaying, from trees. In the backyards people kept chickens, pigs, an occasional goat, and in the vast, swampy side lots there were abandoned bits of plumbing.

The narrow, three-story house badly needed paint, the kind of place that doesn't have curtains at every window, and where the screen doors don't properly shut. There was an ancient school bus parked in the front yard, its hood up, and newspapers and general trash clung against a picket fence. The house had a wraparound porch; a light bulb was burning in the bedroom just above it.

The naked girl was standing in the window without any expression on her face, without any expression at all, and while she was looking down at Senton she didn't move a muscle. He couldn't take his eyes away from her—the large, sloping breasts, the full hips, the white, meaty belly, the coarse tufts of black pubic hair. She suddenly smiled, a removed, inner smile.

Then the pack came around the corner. Senton could smell the wet, acrid fur, the heavy sour breaths. He stepped backwards, into the street, his hands raised to pro-

19

tect his face, but his wife was coming around the corner in the station wagon at the same time, not driving fast but fast enough, and although she wouldn't have had time to brake, she hit him anyway before she saw him, before she realized that anyone was there. When she climbed out of the car, the dogs were standing in a docile circle, partly growling under their breaths, partly ready to wag their tails.

ARTEMIS AND THE JOGGER

A Mild Uproar

Girls are different from women. They rise early, comb their hair, slip into something skimpy, and keep going, as if the world will be less dull when they find what they think they're looking for. You'll notice it's men. The problem is, this college in the heart of America only has boys—high school types who sprawl under cars checking on oil pans. These studs are mothers' sons. They huddle together, nudging each other when something nice goes by, but it's finally all above them. They aren't bookish, and they haven't stumbled onto the sexual revolution. What I'm saying is that, given the situation, I'm kept pretty busy—out there in all hours harvesting alone, rain or shine. I could use an extra man.

When I was still tender, my mother automatically packed me off to a first-class shrink as if she were sending me to a good prep school, something that's done. I put this gentle person at his ease at first, but before we were through he was unbuttoning his coat and loosening his tie; to this day I believe he believes I'm a character who has something coming to him. All right, okay. But when (and if) I ever meet Grief, we'll briefly clasp each other before we go our separate ways—a decent, civilized bargain.

Basically, and without discussing the usual inconsistencies, I am an uncomplicated person, here in this life without a sense of amazement or chagrin. Since I have reached the age of thirty-two with no more than the usual scars, I have managed to hook myself up to the universe without disturbing it, and, in most instances, I can't say that the universe has disturbed me. In any case, I have worked this little fiction out for myself, cut to a comfortable style, and when I shave I like a good cologne, something that stings.

I have a tidy little place in this industrial hamlet in the Middle West, this outpost of ennui. I am comfortably wedged in between a soda shop on my left and a fairy florist on my right, a frustrated decorator who spends his spare time in his sock feet swathed in drapery in his display window, spitting pins and smothering flowers. I carry records, posters and popular paperbacks. I carry a small collection of hard-bound exotic works and the latest in glossy sensitivity cards. In this town it's hardly a living, but I am two blocks from campus, and in all sorts of weather, in all sorts of mental states, I can see the girls going by in the latest cowhide hot pants, top grain. They know they are creating a busy hum; but they still don't know what they're doing, not actually.

A MILD UPROAR

To cut down on costs, I sleep on the premises. The bed back there is always nicely made—a serious little water mattress which sits in its own corner on a plush piece of purple carpet, a bargain. A strobe light, some posters, and a few plastic pillows complete the scene. In the early evening, to freshen things up a bit, a garden hose runs from the sink in the utility, through the store, and into my room where the nozzle fits nicely into the mattress, keeping things gurgling. I'm fueling up, waiting.

I avoid the heavy browsers, the big girls with square, meaty figures down on their knees in army fatigues going through Comparative Religions. I also avoid the tallish pale items, their faces swathed in glassy, semipeaceful expressions, their shawls sweeping the earth while they're on their way toward total understanding, which usually means that some kind of crisis is brewing. I stay away from the divorced, liberated woman with black boots and two children, the former husband behind on the support payments which are putting her through graduate school; and since she wants revenge, a nice male (any male, actually) will do.

I'm interested in the sensitivity card trade—the breezy, freshly minted little juniors with hip-huggers and tank tops who can quote to you with a direct look their favorite lines from Rod McKuen. They specialize in long, breathy silences and tricky ways with their hair. They'll throw their head to one side, as if they're taking in every word, but while the long straight hair swings over the right shoulder, they're watching you watch them. They want to know what's in it for everybody, of course, but we can keep an interesting game going without too much wear and tear.

Cindy Trout first walked into the shop after an exhausting summer in the sun, her hips nuzzling the sand, her transistor blasting, her tote bag crammed with mysterious oils. She's a functionalist's dream: tanned and trim, carved for action; but weary to see fall come.

"It isn't exactly my idea of a great time, being back in this dull town," she observes, thumbing through the sensitivity section.

We get to talking about one thing or another, and pretty soon she admits that she hasn't seen everything; she hasn't seen a water bed before. I fix some instant tea while she prowls around checking out the setup with a suspicious air. "What," she wants to know, knowing, "do you do back here?"

I stir the tea without answering. "Well, what do you think about it, Cindy—the first water bed to grace these parts?"

She tentatively sips the tea. "How do I know the thing's even safe?"

"Try it. Trial by water. We are, in a sense, embarking on a dangerous journey."

"All right, but hold my hand," she orders, removing her shoes.

I figure that she more or less knows what she is doing, but she sits down cautiously, on the edge, while keeping her back straight, her knees together—a close to impossible balancing act when you consider all the undulation going on under her. "Like this?" she asks, innocently, eyeing me.

A MILD UPROAR

"Not exactly."

"What if I spill the tea?"

"Let me take the cup."

She stood up instead. "What's fascinating, really, is what happens when you get off. The thing still joggles, like it's alive. Ugh."

I forgot about Cindy. I am perfectly content to allow into my universe here and there a lost cause; but I should have known better. She appeared again after hours on a sopping night in early fall; leaves were coming unglued before their time, lying plastered against the sides of brick buildings, too soggy to care. Cindy herself was dissolved in tears. She was standing in the doorway and crying like crazy, having a perfectly authentic slump.

I unbuttoned her coat and found some sherry in the bottom of a bottle, enough for a glass. She was wearing a black wool turtleneck; her damp blonde hair was pulled back behind her ears, giving her a certain ragged gravity— an old woman of eighteen.

"I have troubles," she said, "with *boys*."

"Listen, stranger, try the sherry; it's warming."

"I don't want to be warm. I want to be the way I am. Furious, just *furious*," she said, trying the sherry.

"So just relax," I suggested, "because it's raining harder."

Cindy curled up onto the water mattress without counting on its healing powers, and when she calmed down, she looked surprised. "Oh, Charles, what am I *doing* here? What did I ever want to go to college for? I'm not even *majoring* in anything. Daddy set everything up. It's all *his* fault."

"Cindy," I said, pausing, wondering myself what the oracle was going to bring, "existence is an answer to be lived, not a question to be asked."

She looked at me with perfectly wordless admiration, and I wondered then, just for a moment, if I shouldn't drive her home while I still could; but I didn't. While it continued to thrash around outside, a kind of lull settled down within, a nice, friendly numbness. We finally huddled together that night, skin to skin, a circle of comfort against the jokes of life.

I was up and down with Cindy, a smart girl, and I won't say that I didn't have a good thing going. I did. She was cozily made, quite a big girl for a little girl, and she admired older men, somebody with dreams, but I kept both eyes open. I'll admit that girls often live generously, as if there is no tomorrow, but of course there is: it's me.

Her father is a successful electrical contractor down the line, where Indiana and Kentucky stare at each other across the river without speaking. From his porch he can see the Ohio at night and the strings of lights across it which are Louisville—his empire, to hear him talk. He knows every street, has wired every house, and can tell you what fuse is going to go next.

However, power-happy people usually put me to sleep, and while I half dozed on his porch, he planned my future: a chain of first-rate book shops that would materialize

A MILD UPROAR

overnight, taking by surprise the good citizens of Louisville. He was a great reader himself.

"They could use some intellectual stimulation," he
pointed out, as if he were discussing his electrical circuits.

"Oh, *Daddy*," Cindy said, planning my future herself,
"there you go again. Charles doesn't *want* a huge operation. He couldn't keep his eye on things."

"But that's what happens in this country, baby. When
you make money, money comes," he concluded, trailing
off with an air of resignation, a tender but fated capitalist.

Cindy squeezed my hand. She had her ways of handling
her father, but she seldom argued with him about progress
—a muscled, winged creature which had gradually carried
him up over the fuse boxes in Louisville until he was high
on his hill, a battered veteran of dreams.

"Son," he said, "you haven't even had a chance to see
the layout here. Why, I could use a good, strong, mature
male just to keep the grass down."

Cindy's father knew she needed an older man, somebody to take charge. I could see the wedding reception:
everybody celebrating my getting into the Pepsi generation, at a price. Guests hug the punch bowl in panic. Fat
strawberries, out of season and amazed to be there, bump
together in the tidal swell like cash in the bank.

Cindy and I took late autumn strolls through woods filled
with dusty foliage, drying stream beds, and twiggy short-
cuts.

"Cindy, honey," I finally said, "I've got something to

tell you. I caught you on the rebound, and you may not know what you're doing. I was a port in a storm, and that was a pretty rainy night. You've got to be sure. So does your dad. He doesn't know everything about me, either."

"Charles," she said, "what are you trying to tell me? What do you want to do for the rest of your life? Live in that hole behind the store like a mole? What do you ever think of besides your water bed?"

"You're assuming I'm a shallow person."

"I'm assuming what I'm assuming. You'll drive a girl crazy, up to a point, and then you want everybody to straighten up, is that it? Well, I'm walking out of your life," she said—and almost did.

Winter came. Snow dropped and disappeared. Cars skidded across glassy intersections. Girls in heavy, dragging coats briefly discovered an oasis on the water bed, a perfectly comfortable piece of real estate on frozen nights.

Business was good. I packed and unpacked for the seasonal trade. I couldn't keep ahead of things, and cartons began to pile up. While I held a sandwich in one hand, I arranged the merchandise. I was gradually getting a heavier, more mystical customer, and I was ordering items which dealt with God, death, sex, and microbiotic diets.

When we had a few bright days toward the end of March, Cindy suddenly turned up again in the unexpected thaw, a vision among melting car hoods and dripping porch roofs.

She was going with a different crowd. Tall, gangly, gentle, vaguely unfocused young males. Gentle. Gentle. They don't want anything. They usually don't even *say* anything. A new wave of gentle, nonjudgmental types has set in. A new wave of ancient wisdom has set in. On the other hand, considering grass, it may be merely cerebral atrophy, irreversible shrinkage of the brain tissues which causes various neurological symptoms—a condition also frequently found among people who sit around in old folks's homes. They mulled about for awhile, picking up books and putting them down.

Cindy was wearing expensive leather fringe. She was still Cindy Trout, a girl hopelessly torn between home economics and physical education. "Charles," she said, "I was wrong, wasn't I? Really, *really* wrong."

"How's your father?" I finally asked; and, considering the new situation, I was actually curious.

"George?" she said, studying the question as if she were trying to remember just who he was. "Oh, George is George, I guess, Charles. But I'm wondering if I'm hearing what you're really asking. What you're *really* asking. I'm wondering if we could be honest."

Should I play the game? Why not play the game? I didn't play the game. I was happy enough without her new troubles. Too many in my life were already filling the void. I shook my head. "I suppose," I said, "you've gotten it all together, haven't you?"

She looked at me for a minute, suspiciously. "How do you know that I haven't?"

I was still talking to Cindy when her crowd reached the

door without having bought anything—the whole clump moving with the slow, gentle slouch of grazing animals. They stared at Cindy for a minute. When the leader said, "Coming?" she said, "Go ahead, I'll catch up with you," and then the door shut behind them.

We were beginning again. In a sense. Off and on. She was actually pretty busy. She wanted to try grass. So, I said, try grass. What do you want me to do, go up the wall? However, I wouldn't let her try grass in my home, which is my business, and when she wanted to smoke she found her own friends.

George C. Trout must have been picking up the vibrations because he got me on the phone. "Son," the father said, in essence, "I want my little girl to settle down."

Cindy was getting ready for bed. She usually had a Coke late at night, and while she combed her long, reddish blonde hair the Coke bottle stood on the edge of the bureau. She was wearing a green cotton pullover and bikini panties but the long, loose pullover just covered her small bottom. When I hung up, she stopped combing for a minute to ask me a question. She was still looking into the mirror. "Charles," she said, "do you really get along with everybody?"

What was she asking? What was she *really* asking? "Good Lord, no. Where did you get that idea?"

She sipped the Coke for a minute and then put the bottle back down on the bureau. She was combing her hair again, her head to one side. "I wish," she said, "I didn't have to comb this dumb hair all the time."

A MILD UPROAR

She was a little mystery, a perfect puzzle, but a man can't be on his guard every minute. He has to keep up with the world, too.

The local Baptists were picketing a theater which showed X-rated adult films. The manager was letting anyone in free who crossed the picket line. "I can keep it up as long as they can," official sources quoted him as saying. Perhaps he could. On the other hand, the Baptists are a hardy bunch. I wouldn't want to be a hero. The letters of outrage poured into the daily press. I followed the news with some interest, and after about a month's struggle, he briefly landed up in court.

The general excitement stirred the town; business was brisk; the store was filled, as if money had to be out milling around; and while I was busy Cindy appeared with several friends—a child in a forest, an impression of innocence among beards, hair, surplus clothes. They were actually a little more animated than usual. They were carrying a huge carton. Heading toward the rear of the store, my home, my castle, my lair. I have this strong tendency toward closure, and as soon as I could I got back there.

They were carefully unpacking an enormous wedding cake, a classical work with red, white, and blue roses, sugary silver bells, the Parthenon in tiers. The bride-and-groom dolls were standing stiffly at attention under the trellis like a dance team in a 1930s musical.

I stood there for a moment without saying anything. I know how curious life is, and whenever I can avoid it, I don't ask questions; but I have my weak periods. "Where did that come from? Who got married, anyway, a four-star general?"

Two boys, one on each side, were trying to ease it down onto the floor. The third stood watching. "Everybody's getting married today, man. Wow, really, the whole human race. What else can you do with something like this on your hands?"

That's the trouble with the young these days. They think they've got to live symbolic lives. I was busy. I wasn't getting married. I'm also a pretty conventional person, a reflective child of the dying middle class when it comes right down to it, and I wasn't entirely happy about having such hot merchandise on the premises. "Well, be careful back here, please, will you?"

Cindy was looking for plates, napkins, forks. She stared at me for a moment without speaking. Why couldn't she have her little friends back here? I didn't have any hold on her, did I? I didn't *want* any hold on her, did I?

One of the boys was trying to get the trellis loose from the cake. "We wanted to get a *birthday* cake, but we couldn't find what we were looking for—not on the spur of the moment we couldn't, not around here. She's going to be nineteen," he said, busy with the bride-and-groom dolls, trying to find a place to put them.

I had to get to work. I went to the bank around noon, and because I felt curiously depleted I stopped to have a drink or two on my way back. While I was sitting in the bar, I seriously thought about Cindy, and while I was still under this blurred feeling of warmth I thought about getting her an engagement ring; but I finally bought her a

A MILD UPROAR

nice imitation opal pendant. It wasn't inexpensive, either. "Cindy," I wrote on the card, "you're the warm nymph in my elfin grot, a constant consolation in a cold water bed." While I walked back to work, my own imagery began to ferment. I would be lonely without her, I really would. I couldn't say that I wouldn't.

The stereo was blasting in the store. Somebody was playing the same rock piece over and over. The place was dangerously packed. Customers wandered back from the front to have a piece of wedding cake, sometimes staying, sometimes wandering out again. A scattered collection of fraternity brothers was trying to elbow its way through the crowd, and while each carried his own bottle in a brown paper sack, they were beginning to get belligerent.

While I was trying to get to the back of the store to get to the bottom of this, a huge, bearded man in his early sixties grabbed my arm. "Peace," he said, and when I didn't answer, he tightened his grip. "Peace," he said, *"right?"* I nodded. He let go. "Whose party is this, anyways?" he asked, swaying a little from side to side.

Cindy and the boys were sitting cross-legged around the remains of the wedding cake as if around a dying campfire. They were gravely passing a joint around the circle. A woman in a shawl was sitting in a corner with a baby on her lap. She was feeding the baby bits of cake. The baby was concentrating on each bite, opening his mouth before the food reached it. Every once in a while the mother wiped his mouth and chin. "That's a good boy," she kept saying, "that's a good, good boy."

How was I feeling? How was I *really* feeling? I was furious—just furious. "I haven't asked you for very much, Cindy. Have I asked you for very much? I have merely asked that you wouldn't smoke grass back here, in my home, which is my business. Why, I can smell it up there in the store."

Cindy considered me from a grave distance, a long way off. "Charles, I wanted us to come to something, I really did, but I know now what's been wrong with the relationship from the beginning. I'm too old for you," she said.

The scuffle started in the front of the store and then spread, books going over down the line, but when the police cars started to blare in the streets several blocks away, the place emptied in five minutes. When the local officials hoisted themselves up out of their shiny Dodges, I was standing in the shambles trying to spray a little Air Wick around.

"Well, Charles," the sheriff said, not happy, not unhappy, "Have you been having a little difficulty here? Have you got it straightened out yet?"

Oh yes, I said, I had, I had.

The sheriff nodded, not happy, not unhappy. He looked around him for a minute. He finally picked up one of the books from the scattered heap on the floor. "You've got a lot of reading matter around here," he grunted. He removed his sunglasses. He screwed his little eyes up. He was thumbing through *Sacred Erotic Art Through the Ages*, and whenever he came to a glossy illustration he cleared his throat.

"You'll find that an interesting work, sheriff. The world

A MILD UPROAR

of lust is the world of innocence, a blind energy striving forward as if it had somewhere to go. While we study these twisting Indian couples who are bent into such curious shapes, we suddenly realize that we are confronting the modern experimental imagination again: 'Let's just see now . . . where do these parts go? How does everything fit?' "

He tapped the book gravely, thrice. "What else do you have around here like this?"

"Like what?"

"Like this smut, this valuable evidence," he intoned, finally happy.

The two other storm troopers lifted the curtain which separates the store from the water bed. The woman was still feeding the baby bits of cake. The baby opened his mouth wide to take a bite before it got there, but when he saw the men he paused for a moment and then munched slowly, as if he were showing them how to do it.

Everybody wanted to know if this was a place of business, a permanent residence, or both. They wrote something down and then left, their big Dodges heading back downtown as if they couldn't wait another minute to get there.

I tossed and turned for three months. I could get no succor from the water bed. I churned the troubled waters beneath me into a froth.

I talked to myself. "Charles," I said, "where are we going to end up?"

I got no answer. The question was not merely meant as an elegant rhetorical stance, either. I was genuinely interested.

The preliminary hearing lasted ten minutes. "What is he doing," the judge asked my attorney, mildly curious, "flooding the town with trash?"

My attorney politely yawned behind his hand. "Your Honor," he said, "I hope to prove that this harmless collection of pictures is merely a work of art."

The judge wasn't so sure just how harmless art was. "You know," he said, shaking his head as if in admiration and looking at me, the trash peddler, for a moment, "I never saw a book like this before."

We left the sweaty chambers. My attorney hurried down the steps two at a time. He paused for a moment to discuss my future just outside the men's room door. "Charles," he said, "they know this case shouldn't have even come this far. We'll take a light fine without a fight just to keep the city fathers happy, but in the meantime we've got to get you a license to run an adult bookstore. You'll have to call yourself an adult bookstore, though: nobody admitted under twenty-one. Well, after all, why not? You'll get to appreciate a little more mature trade, if you'll give yourself half a chance."

I went home to think about it. I brooded. I wrote Cindy a letter to try to get my thoughts in order, but I finally tore it up. "Cindy," I said, in those fragments, "you're a free woman. I'm a free man, too—free to wonder what freedom means, which is a restriction. I probably won't see

A MILD UPROAR

you again. They'll have an adult bookstore sign over my place, which means no children, and, child, I'm going to miss the children: girls like you with shiny morning faces wanting to know what the world's like, and will they be able to swim with the tide? Well, I was a good instructor, of a sort, but I'm evidently still making payments on the water bed. Which also makes me a student. A student of what? I'm not so sure, but I don't blame you. When you grow up, duck under the adult sign some day and come in. I'll have tea waiting, and you can explain."

I saw Cindy on campus once or twice with a new friend, a young man who did drugs for years, but who is now a Jesus Freak. Here in the middle of the Bible Belt people have no use for Jesus Freaks, and Parker appears to walk in isolated splendor, possibly because he is so tall. The signs of his conversion are evident. He now looks a little more like everybody else. He still has his lengthy, matted hair, but his skin looks better and his eyes are clear. Cindy was wearing something baggy and flowing. I thought about her birthday present, the opal pendant which was still around the store somewhere, but she probably has little use for the baubles of the world these days—at least not now, on this middle rung toward the next interesting upheaval.

The Greening
of Rushville,
Indiana

Midwestern girls tend to be hefty through the hip, solid-bottomed, and small-breasted; but these hard little breasts have an intelligence of their own; they stand up and watch back. Sandy has long dark hair and a slightly Jewish face; but she has Indian cheekbones. She is from Rushville, Indiana, Wendell Willkie's old hometown, his stamping grounds. Sandy's parents (WASPs who own the Rushville Ford agency) attend something called the Plum Rose Christian Church. Plum Rose theology stresses a primitive, back-to-the-roots form of Christianity, and, ignoring the more recent rebellions, it doesn't call itself Protestant. The church members celebrate a weekly but symbolic Communion, practice total immersion, and wash feet on special occasions.

What does Sandy Blattner believe? You know the story: a middle-class girl, what she wants to do is to start living.

THE GREENING OF RUSHVILLE, INDIANA

Sandy has heard about the Sexual Revolution (those salty, stirring tides), but she believes that she's a landlocked child who is merely listening to its gentle persuasions from a great distance.

In any case, she's also confused about her sexual convictions because she has gotten into the women's liberation literature. She has to talk about it, and, sitting in my office between classes, she ponders and ponders. She is wearing a tank top and tight white denims. She is shy and soft-spoken. She speaks slowly and hesitantly because she's constantly waiting to be interrupted to be told she's wrong.

She is sitting sideways across from my desk in the cramped office space, and when she turns to face me, her hair swings slightly. "Well, you know," she says, "I really understand what *The Second Sex* means when it talks about sexual intercourse . . ."

She pauses, thinking. She moves her hair away from the side of her face with the edge of her hand. I wait, interested.

"That sexual intercourse is like a territorial invasion for the woman? But I'm so *ambivalent* about it, too," she concludes, in despair, "because I think it's neat to have it in me . . ."

She pauses. She blushes for a moment, but I have misunderstood the cause; and when she looks up again she says: "Horrors! Please forgive the old-fashioned slang, *neat!*"

A man must have his moral imperatives, these little tricks and balancing acts. (Morality is a form of theater, anyway.) I am not more complex than most, but I do not touch a student while she is officially registered in one of my classes. Sandy is. She is currently attending my Literature and Modern Living 301; but Literature and Modern Living is rapidly drawing toward the end of the academic quarter (ready to die on its feet, in fact), and while I wait for its sweet demise (freeing me to tie her), I am willing to play the counseling game.

I try to put her at her ease, which is not easy. "Well, whether it's old-fashioned or not, I think that *neat* is still a neat word."

She sits there, worrying. "Do you?" she says, not listening. The insecure have their own way of not hearing; they are tuned in to an inner voice which keeps them hopping; what, in another context, has been called a different drummer. "Anyway," she finally says, "I'm very confused, I guess."

I am still willing to hear about her loneliness without climbing over the desk to cup her rump against my palms; but at the same time I have got to be careful that my colorless professional responses don't forever cook my goose —don't ruin my chances when Literature and Modern Living 301 has gracefully passed on, when the grades are safely tucked away in the registrar's files where they can doze undisturbed in their purity through everybody's eternity.

"It's natural, Sandy, a very warm girl like you," I suggest, letting through, you will notice, this modest modicum of lust.

"Well, you wouldn't *believe* Rushville if you *saw* it."

THE GREENING OF RUSHVILLE, INDIANA

"Rushville?"

"The place where I grew up. It must be the heart of the heart of alienation," she concludes, having picked up the "heart of the heart" bit from another writer, this time a midwestern male.

I'm a curious man. I'm given to toying with temptations without actually succumbing, a dangerous business for some. "I'd like to see Rushville."

For a moment, in silence, she searches my face to find the meaning, and while she stews over the problem, she finds everything there but the meaning. "Would you? *Really? Why?*" Then she finally relaxes and deflates. "Oh, you're being *ironic*, I'm so dumb," she concludes, half happy.

"What about this weekend?"

She sighs. "Well, all right, if you say so, but you don't know what you're getting into," she observes; and, the truth is, I don't.

When the weekend appeared, we went down to Rushville —a ripe happening because that year the early May weather suddenly burst into three days of midsummer warmth; and everything was coming out or trying to come out at once. Trees make a hometown. Here and there the massive foliage which filters the sun hurts the front lawns, darkens the parlors inside in midday, and holds the damp in the sexy summer evenings when the streetlights come on. Main is lined with two- and three-story frame houses with tall, narrow windows, some semi-interesting gingerbread, a few nice gables, and those wraparound porches with wooden swings on chains. A Gothic mansion with turrets and a wide circular drive has become a funeral home; but along its porch the garden beds blaze with tulips—any bulb being death's comedown.

It's Sandy's aliveness that is beginning to tell. She has washed her hair and pulled it back, just behind the ears, which emphasizes the long, lean cheekbones; and she is wearing a demure minidress, a little less brief than usual because we are visiting her folks, the Plum Rose Christians.

"I want to see the tree that's growing up out of the courthouse roof."

"The tree? What tree? Oh, you mean in Greensburg. That's down the line."

(Certain items need changing. When I write about this, I'll put the tree in Rushville, take out the humming Ford agency and ignore the atypical Catholic church which sits on Main, more or less happy, across from a First Christian.)

But I like the dusty, defunct-looking Dairy-Whip which is packing them in in the middle of this white noon light. The adolescents there are seldom driving cars less than two years old; the bustle among the vehicles has a ritualistic tang.

Sandy's folks live on a hot-looking side street in a two-story split-level which is half wood and half something else which could be stone but probably isn't. The house has a raw look; the yard hasn't been settled on yet; and there are

THE GREENING OF RUSHVILLE, INDIANA

several mounds of expensive-looking compost piled up here and there in the dirt. Somebody has bought a tree. "That's going to be a poplar," she says while we're on the new cement walk, which looks as if it has recently been swept.

Sandy's baby sister, a high school cheerleader with some local fame, abruptly opens the front door, ready to get an early view. She is drawing this day to a close in pale blue hotpants and strong-looking little bare feet. She scuffs backwards onto the cold tile in the entranceway. "I didn't know you were coming," she says to Sandy, knowing everything, of course.

Sandy hurries through the introduction. Since we have arrived, her general insecurity has obviously picked up speed. "Where's the family?" she asks, ready to get the greetings concluded in one swoop.

"They aren't here. George is in the cellar."

"On a day like this?"

"What kind of day is it?"

"Hot," I say, looking Bambi over. She is small but joyfully put together—somebody who is going to become somebody's sweet ache, if she already hasn't.

"Let's take him into the family room. They aren't there, either."

Sandy hesitates. She gives her sister a swift, uncertain look. "Oh, all right, I'll meet you there. Be sure you're there. I'm going to get my brother," she says, heading toward the rear of the house.

The chintz-covered family room is filled with glossy duplications of Early American tables, chairs, and TV sets. Here and there the bowls of glass fruit sparkle darkly in isolated splendor. Norman Rockwell-like illustrations are humming on the walls, those smooth, pallid depictions of a mythical Hoosier world: red barns and covered bridges, big-rumped work horses in harness, little girls in sunbonnets and freckle-faced boys carrying fishing poles. The room as a whole seems to be in a curious flux. I pick the couch because it looks steady, but when I sit down even that rocks.

Bambi curls up on the opposite end of the couch, her eyes focused on her bare toes, and for a moment, a fleeting moment, I catch in the expression her sister's favorite, faraway look.

"Sandy tells me that Rushville is a lonely place."

Bambi glances up. "She did, did she? Well, we keep busy," she says, absently—probably thinking about the ways she keeps busy.

"Fine, fine."

"We cure it in the abandoned barns around here."

"Loneliness?"

"No, crazy! Grass. Good, home-cured Hoosier grass."

"Pot?"

She stretches in her pullover, yawning, showing a bit of hard, bare belly, a regular little Hoosier cheerleader type. "Are you *really* a college professor?"

"In loose terms, yes."

She ponders this for a moment, as if she is wondering just what these loose terms may mean. "George is a high school dropout," she says, proudly, obviously considering George to be the success in the family.

"What does he do in the cellar?"

"That's a long story."

Sandy and George appear. He is wearing cut-down denims but no shirt, and he is mostly bone. His hair covers his head and his neck like a woolly ball, a kind of fuzzy, half-tangled yarn. He peers at me during the introduction as if he is trying to place the face, but he gives Bambi the same look. He places in my hand a cool, feathery clasp and then steps back to let somebody else say something, if somebody else wants to say something.

Both girls look nonplused. Making conversation (or trying to), I ask him what line he's in.

He seems to be considering the possibilities for a moment. He finally says, "Electrical appliances," abruptly.

Bambi looks at Sandy. "He's kidding. He's an electronic genius."

He appears to be taking this in. He excuses himself, on his way back to the cellar.

The place is suddenly quiet, as if an unfortunate lapse has briefly descended on an otherwise stirring conversation.

Bambi looks at Sandy again. She tells me that George is busy on a remote-controlled dildo that pulsates with a flesh-like warmth and murmurs, "I love you, I love you" during its final stages of ecstasy.

I didn't believe it. Did I believe it?

A car door slams. Bambi briefly stirs. "Oh, God, here he is, the beast returns."

The groceries fill the doorway first. *Angst*-ridden, guilt-propelled, Sandy jumps up to help her parents with the supermarket shopping; but everybody finally follows their trail back into the magnificent, two-toned kitchen with its bewildering array of push buttons and built-in appliances. An immense picture window faces more dirt in the backyard.

The parents gradually lower the groceries down onto the table. They are arguing about the shopping, and amidst the general confusion, Sandy gets started on the final introductions.

Mr. Blattner has a huge, hard gut, like a workingman's, but the distinguished-looking, silvery gray hair is distracting. He is still muttering over the groceries when he holds out his big hand. "The fucking prices they charge for everything these days," he says, and then, without pausing, he takes Bambi in. "Aren't you going to get any clothes on?"

Bambi looks at him for a moment without speaking. "These are clothes," she says, in an absolutely flat tone.

Mrs. Blattner has plugged in the electric teflon skillet, and while she dips the parts of chicken into the cornmeal, she moves her hair away from her forehead with the side of her arm. She is a fatty little woman, with pale, absent-looking eyes. "Where's George?" she asks, probably to herself, probably without really wanting to know.

Bambi is busy opening a Coke. "Where do you think? Downstairs, working on his dildo."

Mrs. Blattner evidently doesn't know what a dildo is.

THE GREENING OF RUSHVILLE, INDIANA

"Well, he's got to eat, doesn't he, and I bought this nice fresh chicken."

We eat fried chicken in the kitchen, framed in the big picture window. While we're sitting down, Sandy and Mrs. Blattner are trying to find room for the mashed potatoes, the baking-powder biscuits, the bowls of brown gravy, the potato salad, the string-bean salad, and the beet salad.

Blattner finally lowers his silvery head. "O Lord, we ask that Thou breathe upon this our family and upon this our food Thy blessings. Amen. Young man, will you start the chicken around."

The steaming food raises the temperature in the room. The air-conditioning isn't working right, and the last of the day's heat has crept around to the back, where it can assault the picture window.

Blattner can't find the apple butter. While Sandy jumps up to get it, the father leans confidentially across the potato salad. "Tell me," he says, "what do you think about these college riots you've been having?"

He hasn't exactly caught me off-guard. On first sight, any stranger would know that Blattner will want to maul him over playfully until he has gotten a good, solid grip. I do great imitations. I use his wife's look—part absentmindedness, part injured innocence. "Riots? We haven't been having any riots."

"We?"

"Where I'm teaching."

He nods, reflecting. An odd expression crosses his face —something resembling pleasure. "You got a lot of police up there?" he asks, his fork poised in midair.

I switch the subject. I ask him about Wendell Willkie's birthplace.

"*Who?*"

Just then the lights go off and then come back on with a humming sound.

Blattner puts down his fork. "Is that kid still fooling around down there? Why isn't he up here eating?"

Mrs. Blattner pushes the biscuits back toward me for the third time. "Well," she says to the biscuits, "I've told him about the nice chicken."

Blattner throws her a black glance and gets up. He goes down the hall and opens the cellar door. "George! Your mother wants you to get your ass up here, on the double, which means, in your language, *right now!*"

Nobody answers.

Bambi picks at her plate without actually sitting in her chair. "He's going to have a heart attack one of these days, and fall right down those cellar stairs," she says, cheerfully.

Sandy blots her mouth with a paper napkin. She looks at me nervously. "It's your father, after all," she says, still looking at me, wondering how I am bearing up.

Blattner returns. "*Him?*" Bambi says, surprised.

Blattner turns on her. "Baby sister, I want you to count the number of times I've asked you not to eat in this house standing up. Hard-earned money bought that table, bought that chair."

"I'm late now. I've got to run."

"Where do you think you're going?"

"Out."

THE GREENING OF RUSHVILLE, INDIANA

Blattner thinks he's caught her. He gives her a crafty glance. "And in whose car?"

"You said I could have it tonight."

"Well, your mother and I are going to church."

"*Again?*" she says, looking at her mother.

While delicately chewing, Mrs. Blattner manages to raise one pious brow. Other than this, she doesn't answer. She doesn't ask Bambi where *she's* going. She has learned through the years not to dwell too closely on a lot of things.

"A little bit of church wouldn't hurt you none any, neither," Blattner tells Bambi, threatening.

She doesn't answer. She leaves the table to call a cab.

Mr. and Mrs. Blattner get ready for church. Sandy stacks the dishes in the automatic washer. I hover over her, in the way; but being alone with her at last, after the chaos, has its swift effect. I feel as if I've known her half my life. "I've got to go with them," she tells me, without turning around from the washer, "because I never do."

I can feel her hot perplexity in my bones, those helter-skelter hungers which will soon get focused. "That's okay. I'll make out."

"Are you sure?"

"I'll miss you."

She gives me a look while she's drying her hands, as if my interest may be beginning to dawn. "I'll get sick. I get sick whenever I go out with them."

"Then why are you going out with them?"

"I told you. Because I never go out with them," she says, rushing off to change for church.

A screaming car filled with adolescents pulls up in front of the Blattner place, unexpectedly, and Bambi dashes off with them before her cab comes. The parents and their older daughter leave for church. (Sandy casts over her shoulder a final troubled look: Now are you *sure* you'll be all right?) George appears from the cellar. He is still shirtless, but he is now wearing around his neck on a leather thong a huge peace symbol like a small cartwheel. ("Hi," he says, in passing, not really taking me in.) He goes into the kitchen, opens the refrigerator and moves things around in there. While chewing on a chicken leg, he wanders through the house in a sort of trance, picking things up and putting them down.

Bambi's cab stops in front of the house. George finally gets around to answering the doorbell, the chicken leg still in his hand.

The cabdriver stands on the front steps chewing on an unlit cigar. He is wearing a yellow T-shirt and black chino trousers. He is short but stone-solid. He has bulging arms and a huge back. He peers around George into the house, seeing me. He has the sort of mildly inquisitive face that can go sour at a moment's notice. "Somebody here called a cab," he says, ready for an argument—any argument.

George bites into the chicken leg, considering. He turns around to me. I shake my head. He shrugs.

"Now look, friends," the killer says, clearing his throat, "*somebody* in this house has rang for a cab, and *somebody* in this house is going to take a ride, that's a fack. Which one of you is it going to be?"

We decide to go together, George and I, and when we

THE GREENING OF RUSHVILLE, INDIANA

climb into the back of the cab, George is still chewing on his chicken leg, his big bare knees drawn up together almost under his chin.

The cabby pulls down the meter handle. "Okay, what's your pleasure? Where's it going to be?"

George and I look at each other. We can't think of a thing.

"Come on, come on, friends. This is costing you good money. Where do you want to go?"

George clears his throat. "It's a nice night. Why don't we just drive around?"

"Drive *around?* Drive around *where?* Are you crazy? I tell you what. Would you like a nice piece of ass? I could get you a nice piece of ass."

George agrees. We screech out of the Blattners' drive, cross Main and then disappear in the shadows into a tumble of side alleyways and unpaved streets. Every once in awhile we recross Main. We're finally out into the flat, treeless regions. The driver stops in front of a tall, shuttered farmhouse, but it is unlit. He looks puzzled.

"What the hell," George says, getting slightly aggressive.

The driver checks us out in his rearview mirror. "You people wait here a minute. I'll stir somebody up."

We wait in the cab, watching. The driver knocks on the front door, several times, then goes around to the side and peers through a window. He works his way around toward the back through a tangle of rundown sheds and broken farm machinery. He disappears. How long is he gone? Ten minutes? Fifteen?

He finally appears, coming around the side of the house

51

shaking his head. "I can't find *nobody*," he says, climbing into the cab. "So? Where to now?"

Silence.

"All right, all right, I'll tell you what I'd be willing to do. Since it's my mistake—right?—I'll give you a good blow job myself. Five bucks a head, money-back guarantee."

I clear my throat. "I've been wanting to see Wendell Willkie's old home ever since I came to town."

The man brightens. "The former Republican presidential candidate? Sure thing," he says, glad to be tearing out of there.

We come back into town. We take a few sharp turns past some big homes, but he is obviously playing guessing games, and he gives up. When we finally reach the Blattners' place, he is crestfallen, almost human. He can't be sorry enough. He is still trying to apologize while George pays him off at the door.

"Listen, just let me give you a call around Friday, next Friday . . ."

The Blattners have by this time come back from church. We can hear them arguing in low tones in the back bedroom. George turns in. Bambi is not in yet. Sandy is in the bathroom, vomiting, and when she appears, she is as white as a sheet. "I'm sorry," she says, passing me in the hall on her way to bed, "but I *told* you I'd be sick."

I'm sympathetic. Aren't I sympathetic? I give her a sympathetic look.

The adolescents finally roar up. The front door opens, then slams shut. While I'm turning down the covers in the

THE GREENING OF RUSHVILLE, INDIANA

guestroom, Bambi knocks on the door and then opens it a crack. She stands there piercing me with that telltale stoned look. "Do you have everything you need?" she asks.

I have a bad night. First, Bambi appears. She is in a brief metallic-looking outfit which glitters when she moves. When she reaches the center of the floor, she twirls these blazing batons—throwing them up into the air and then passing them back and forth between her legs. I am conscious of a huge crowd but I can't see it. I have a cigarette somewhere in my pockets but I can't locate a match. I am rolling around in an enormous, open field with Bambi, Sandy, and Mrs. Blattner—soundless, flavorless goings-on, actually; but Mr. Blattner suddenly appears in his nightshirt, trying to bat us all apart with a huge pair of velvet house slippers. He finally raises the slippers in a kind of benediction. "The fucking prices you pay for everything these days," he says, and disappears. I am in a car in the dark alone—going around and around and around trying to find Wendell Willkie's old home.

The spring quarter draws to a close. The dorm roofs are now filling up with sunbathing girls. While I lecture, I watch Sandy in the front row now and then. She is steadily growing deep brown, her small breasts berry-crisp in the tight white sleeveless top. She seldom looks up. She is busy-busy taking notes, and when the bell rings, she is the first to leave. I can't keep my heavy heart from wandering toward that disappearing rump; but at the same time I am partly relieved that she doesn't turn up in the office these days, because I am beginning to believe that I can't make it through her final exams.

She appears in the office during the last week of class. She comes in slowly, wearing shorts and sandals, carrying her books against her breast.

I put down my pen. Why am I worrying so? Isn't she a good student, a sure *B?* In any case, this could be the point, the touchy problem: if I take her right now, while the class is still going, I could change my mind about the *B,* and, overreacting while trying to hold onto a dwindling moral perspective, I just might move her down to a *C* to be on the safe side—the side where the Great Ethical Imperatives stand.

She looks confused and even more uncertain than usual, and when I ask her to sit down, she gives me a totally frank, totally brutal look. "Are you *sure* you want me to?"

"Why? What for heaven sakes is wrong?"

She shrugs, looks away. "Oh—I couldn't face you for awhile, not after that whole Rushville scene."

"Nonsense, Sandy. I've missed you. And very much."

She isn't convinced yet. "Then everything's okay?"

"Everything's great."

She falls into the seat across from me with a great, long-drawn-out sigh, and at the same time—as nude and as lovely as two huge flowers—her eyes begin to widen. Then they are brimming with happy tears. "Oh, I'm *so* relieved. You don't *know* how relieved I am. Because, without asking you, I registered for your Literature and Modern Living 302 this summer, this first quarter."

THE GREENING OF RUSHVILLE, INDIANA

The Man
Who Tried Out
for Tarzan

I am the son of a man who once tried out for Tarzan, and it is, I suppose, my special claim to fame, even if Lex Barker finally got the part. I am not always sure how much I have been affected by all this, and while I have, I certainly have, I'm not going into it—partly because I'm not interesting (I'll be the first to admit), and partly because it's my business.

If you want to hear my father tell about the trip to Hollywood and the screen test, you take Route 95 out of New Haven, stay on 95 past Guilford, and get off at Madison. My father and his third wife live back in North Madison among the trees and the advertising executives, but on weekends, from April through the early part of November, depending upon the weather, you will generally find him in the water, down off the Madison beach.

He will be the one going around and around out there

in one of those little, flat-bottomed sailboats which isn't much bigger than a surfboard, even when, in November, the small-craft warnings are usually up, and he is out there alone. He once swam on a college swimming team, and when the wind gets too rough, when he can't handle the tender little craft any longer, he jumps overboard, puts the rope between his teeth, and brings her back in. He once got caught in a gale, and when he finally crawled out on all fours under a clear sky, he ran into a nest of Wellesley girls who were picnicking on the sand. They shared their hot coffee with him—the faint echo of old Odysseus there, part of his Old-World flavor, the gentleman who reads, although for a living he sells oil. He *has* a gentlemanly air which, while not poured on, is always there, or certainly always there around women.

He is a huge, barrel-chested man in his early fifties, and although he has a big middle now, it is still fairly hard gut. He has small, tight, graying ringlets which run down the back of his neck and jus⁺ over his ears. The shirt, open across the chest, exposes that same tight, springy stuff, like steel wool. When he is sailing, he usually wears ragged knee-length shorts held up around the heavy middle with rope, the shorts bagging in back across the small buttocks, and I still like to picture his coming up out of the surf in this costume and then charming those college kids: asking names, complimenting, noticing little things, like the color of some rather plain girl's hair. The trouble is, he finally doesn't care . . .

My wife came from the Midwest—one of those vast, square, inland states which the average easterner associates with nothing at all, but when I brought her back to New England to meet him, he immediately said: "Beautiful swimmers you have out there, perfectly beautiful swimmers," as if Mary Ann were personally responsible for the swimming, but five minutes later, when we were walking toward the house, he couldn't remember her name.

The house is a big, impressive, four-bedroom Cape Cod. My father puts a lot of stock in appearances. He once drove a small blue Mercedes, but when he suddenly found himself out of work, he went out and purchased a large white Mercedes—following the theory that you can't let people know you're down when you're down.

Jane, my father's wife, was on her knees in front of the house. She was digging in a garden, or, rather, she was trying to *make* a garden, a place to lay a few fall bulbs to rest. "But it's all just *builder's* sand!" she said, pointing with her small, insufficient-looking trowel. Jane was in her early forties. She was still an attractive woman, in that pale, wide-eyed way, and her reactions, despite the accumulating years, suggested a young girl's innocence, or blankness. She implied that everything got ahead of her; outmaneuvered or outfoxed her in one way or another.

My father was standing behind her. "That's symbolic, isn't it—no dirt?" he said, his literary mind at work again. He was originally from Upstate New York, and although he has lived so long in New England he says *soca* for *soccer* but *idear* for *idea*, he was evidently still wondering if he was paying for the *real*, the *authentic*, New England or not.

He caught me looking at him. He shook his head and

finally introduced his wife. During the flurry of cross-introductions that followed, Jane said to me (while looking at Mary Ann, my bride), "Oh, *Charles*, she is *so* lovely, isn't she?" as if it were a cry of despair. Then the two women embraced in a brief, hard way before they stood apart, without anything else to say.

My father stirred. "Well? Shall we go see if we can find ourselves a drink?"

The two divorces had made brutal inroads on his income, and if you couldn't have known this from the outside of the house, the big, hollow interior showed it: a huge, curved couch and a few really good Early American pieces, but the spacious living room was still half bare, like a polished shell. They had put the bulk of his ravaged income on the Cape Cod itself, planning to pick up furniture as they could, and because they were not young, there was something particularly touching about this tentative hopefulness.

My father himself moved through a richer, denser element of his own creating—his elusive sense of reality which suggested that he was of course *camping out*, on his way to more meaningful places. "What're we drinking these days?" he said to me, as if he were prepared to offer anything, but he added, "What about bourbon? We have bourbon," he said, without looking at his wife, "and—I think, Jane?—beer?" He was looking at Jane now. She said nothing. "That is, of course, unless Jane's already gotten into the last of the beer."

Mary Ann and I were sitting alone on the huge couch, almost out of contact with the rest of the room, but the

THE MAN WHO TRIED OUT FOR TARZAN

tense air out there, around the two, was unmistakable. I realized just *who* had actually finished the beer.

Jane looked at him without expression, but while he was rattling around with the glasses in the kitchen, a small blue Persian cat suddenly appeared and jumped up into her lap. She held her arms up away from her body until the creature had finally curled into its chosen position. "Crazy animal," she said, stroking him. "You *are* just a *crazy* animal, aren't you?" She looked up at us, wearing that wide, helpless, abashed look. "We can't let him out. He literally goes *crazy* when he sees the trees."

My father came back carrying everything on an ornate round silver tray—glasses, soda, ice cubes, a pitcher of water, and a freshly opened bottle of bourbon. He stood in the middle of the sparsely furnished room holding the tray and looking from side to side, wondering where he was going to put it. I got up to help, but he said: "Sit still, sit still," in his abrupt, impatient way. He saw the milking stool that was standing beside the fireplace, and while he was still holding the tray, he edged the stool out toward the center of the room with his foot.

"That tray," Jane said, "won't balance on that stool."

He ignored her. On his haunches, concentrating on what he was doing, he lowered the tray down on the stool, and, still on his haunches, he took our orders. When we had our drinks, he poured himself a generous-sized glass half full, and without mixing it, or adding ice, he took his first tentative sip—a man who can afford to have just a sip because he's got a lot more there.

He finally looked up at us on the couch, pleased. "Well,

Jane," he said, without looking at her, "what do you think of the bourbon?"

Jane shifted her weight in the chair, and the cat jumped off her lap. "You know what I'm thinking," she said.

Mary Ann leaned forward, unaware of the crosscurrents between the husband and the wife. In fact, she didn't understand *him* at all. He was a puzzle. She had that careful, slightly touchy manner of someone who is always waiting not to understand what is going on, but at the same time he will pursue the matter as best he can, at whatever the cost.

"Why?" Mary Ann asked Jane. "Don't you like bourbon?"

My father winked at me. He turned the radio dial past a World Series game (a decisive one), and when he found the Saturday afternoon opera, he adjusted it low. "We have to flip back every once in awhile to pick up the baseball scores," he said. "Jane *likes* that commercialism."

Mary Ann cleared her throat, ready to begin the leading sentence, the business of the afternoon. "Charles tells me you were almost in a Tarzan movie once," she said.

I have since been divorced, and the whole afternoon, from this safe distance, seems curiously remote, but I had a flashback at that moment, one of those abrupt switches in time and space where, for a second, I was back in our motel room watching Mary Ann try to think. She was standing in the shadowy room in her half slip and bra, absently combing her long blonde hair without looking in the mirror. Her head was slightly to one side, and her hand was holding her hair out as the comb went through it.

THE MAN WHO TRIED OUT FOR TARZAN

"Well," she was saying, "I can't help it, Charles. I just don't get it. Why would anyone want to give up a good college education to play Tarzan?"

I smiled, knowing why. Who wouldn't? "Why don't you ask him?"

However, my father did not answer her. His movements were already growing a little blurred, a trifle off. He finally nodded to himself, as if he were remembering something else, and then he walked into the kitchen. We could hear him going to the bathroom, and then the back door opened. He must have opened it to get some air because he closed it in another moment and came back into the room. He broke into the scattered conversation that was going on between his wife and mine.

"We haven't read that book, have we, dear?" Mary Ann asked me.

I saw my father hesitate, fascinated with her use of the first person plural. He looked at me, as if he were going to comment, but he merely announced that it was drizzling out. Then he sat down heavily in his chair.

Now there were days when he didn't want to talk about himself—rare days, I'll grant, but there were these days, and we had come on one of them. However, I was angry, and I didn't care. I was angry because I suddenly realized I had brought my new bride out to show her off, to get his approval, or, more likely, his envy, and when he merely insisted on seeing her as another woman in his private war, I felt rebuffed, refused. I blushed, like a boy, and, for a brief moment, I crazily wondered if I was supposed to take her back to the Midwest, turn her in, choose another woman, and report here again.

I looked him in the eyes. "I've been saving the Tarzan part for you to tell," I said, without taking my eyes away from his.

He looked at me for a moment and then his glance rested on Mary Ann. I had no idea what he was going to say or do, but then I realized that his brooding expression was beginning to break up and that, in another moment, he was going to realize that she was a pretty woman, wasn't she, and what the hell?

"I'll show you some films," he said.

I had been down this road before, of course, and while he got out the projector, the screen, and the cans of film, I helped his wife to move the furniture around. I have seen the clippings dozens of times—scattered frames taken from his college days showing him swimming, showing him running, showing him posing with the discus and the javelin. These are all lonely ventures, every one, and in the trials of endurance or feats of skill, he is obviously pitting himself against someone else within. He has painfully edited these films over the years until he has eliminated his less flattering angles and positions, and along the way I have also noticed the abrupt disappearance of familiar faces of former mistresses or former friends who had originally appeared on the sidelines. Why were they gone? What had they done to him? What, in each face, did he not want to recall? In any case, he evidently went over and over his past in the films until he had it just the way he imagined it *should* have been.

THE MAN WHO TRIED OUT FOR TARZAN

He always saves the screen-test clips for the Tarzan role until the last, and when the lights came on, he threaded the film through the projector while he explained how two Hollywood scouts had been looking around the eastern college swimming teams, and when they saw him in a tank suit, that was it; they offered him a trip to the West Coast.

Mary Ann sat forward on the edge of the couch, her elbow on her knee, her chin in her hand. She looked impressed and reserved at the same time, as if she were waiting to enjoy the story, to get the point, but when the lights went out again and the film came on, she said, "Oh," in a startled way. "We're going to see the screen test, aren't we? How did you ever get hold of it?"

My father gets dizzy spells these days, and he takes special pills, but in the movie he is going through the air on the end of a rope, and when he lets go, he lands in a wild-enough-looking river somewhere. The rest, the bulk of the short film, was shot in the studio in front of some artificial-looking palms, and when you see the close-ups, you know why he did not get the part. His body may be all right, but his face is not. There is something blurred and sensitive and already bloated in the young face which the heavy, old-fashioned studio makeup merely emphasizes, and while you watch, you are gradually aware that he is trying to *act*. Can you imagine? He evidently *sees* something in Tarzan which no one else has ever noticed before, and while it is partly trapped under the makeup, he is trying to bring it to life.

The lights came on. Jane got up and, bored, fiddled

with the radio dial to get the ball game. Mary Ann merely looked confused.

"Why don't the two of you stay for dinner?" my father said abruptly. "I'll fix my shrimp dish."

Jane turned around, her hand still on the radio dial. "I'm not sure we *have* enough shrimp," she said.

"Oh, hell, yes we have."

I said that we had to get going, but he insisted, and I could not handle his drunken effusiveness. He was tighter than I realized. He had held himself together during the movie, but when he walked now, he was unsteady.

"I *wish*," Jane said, "that you'd at least put some water in the bourbon. I *don't* understand how you can drink it raw."

My father looked at his wife, studying her for a long time, and then he smiled. "That's right. You don't, do you?" he said.

He left the room to get started on the meal, and Jane followed him out. We could hear him fussing over this, fixing that, while they argued in low tones. He finally came back carrying a knife, a head of lettuce, and a wooden salad bowl. He sat down with his things on his lap, his glass beside his chair, and began to cut the lettuce up into big chunks.

Jane got up to answer the phone. She came back. "The cat's out," she said, getting her raincoat. "Somebody let the cat out. He's up in a *tree* across the street."

My father ignored her, as usual. I wasn't sure he had even heard. He was smiling to himself, his head still bent

THE MAN WHO TRIED OUT FOR TARZAN

over the salad bowl. "Oh, hell," he finally said. He was still cutting up the lettuce.

I jumped up to help, and Mary Ann rose, too, and in the general confusion I was going out the front door with the women—women's work, evidently, because my father did not move from his chair.

The neighbor who had called was waiting for us. She stood in the doorway of her place across the street, a raincoat over her shoulders, and her arms across her breast. She pointed. "He's up there," she said. "I saw him come tearing across the yard, and then he just *jumped* into that tree."

Mary Ann, Jane, and I stood in the drizzle in the front yard across the street helplessly looking up into the tree. The drizzle was soft and fine, but my hair was getting soaked, plastered down, and my glasses were streaked. I took my glasses off every once in awhile and wiped them on a damp piece of Kleenex. The woman put the front door light on, but it didn't help much. The tree was partly bare, but there was still enough general foliage that its middle was blurry and dense, and while we could hear the cat crying in the drizzle and the dark, we could not see it.

"Jay's not home," the woman said, "so I don't know what to do."

It was a big tree, not easy to climb. I tried to judge it in the dark. "Do you have a ladder?"

"Do you want a ladder?" the woman said. "I could get a ladder."

Jane was walking in little circles around the tree, trying

to see the cat, and at the same time calling to it. She stopped circling and put her hand on my arm. "Could you get up there, Charles, if we could get a ladder?"

I didn't know if I could reach the cat from the ladder, but I said that I could try. I was going to have to try. "Where's the ladder?" I asked.

The woman didn't want to get wet until she had to. "I'll go through the house and meet you in the garage," she said. "We have a ladder in the garage or somewhere in the cellar."

I started toward the garage, and Mary Ann put her hand on my arm, a tight grip. She was ready to go along. She did not want to be left alone. She was soaked, too, but she didn't want to be left alone with my father in the house, either.

"We'll get the ladder," Jane said. "You two stay here. Keep your eyes on the tree."

"Oh, God," Mary Ann said in a low tone when Jane was gone. "Why do *you* have to get that damn cat down?"

My father appeared. He was still carrying his glass. "Where's everybody?"

"They're looking for a ladder."

"Oh, hell," my father said, "here, hold this."

"But why not wait for the ladder, Dad?"

He didn't answer. He gave Mary Ann his glass, and then, before I could say anything else, he was up in the tree. He got the cat without any trouble, but it screamed terribly, once, and he threw it down, away from him. It landed on its feet, bounced up into the air, and lit out.

THE MAN WHO TRIED OUT FOR TARZAN

We waited for him to come down next, but he didn't. We heard some branches move over our heads, and then a branch cracked, and some stiff little leaves fell. He swore, but then he was still. I asked him if he was all right. "Yes, I'm all right," he said, but his voice sounded low and queer, and I suddenly realized that he couldn't get down. He didn't say anything else. Everything for a minute was quiet up there.

"Well," Mary Ann said, "Mr. McCollister?"

I squeezed her arm, asking her to be quiet. She looked at me with resentment, took her arm away, and rubbed it. "Well?" she said, under her breath, "what did I do?"

Where were the fool women with the ladder? It was drizzling harder now, closer to rain, and getting cold. I told Mary Ann to go back to the house, but she wouldn't budge without me, and I didn't want to leave him up there until the ladder came. I was furious with her, but I couldn't do anything about her now, under the tree, and I realized that, to get her out of there, I was going to have to go away, too.

As it happened, my father could still handle the situation, and while he shifted gears, changing from one myth about himself to another, he settled into the damp foliage. "I never spend *time* in trees anymore," he said. "Why is that? Why do you suppose I don't spend any *time* in trees these days? Who is man? What does he want? Where is he going? Why is everything so rush-rush?"

I was willing to listen, if he wanted to talk. I will admit that the words coming down from the tree in the dark had a certain chilling effect. We pretended, he and I, that he was finally offering me some sound advice, and while he made pronouncements and told lies, he kept his eyes away from the two women who were finally struggling across the lawn through the drizzle with the borrowed ladder.

THE MAN WHO TRIED OUT FOR TARZAN

Tristan

George Trevelyan-Lwyd came on board at the last minute, looking anxious and slightly harried. He was still handsome in his early fifties, but he had spent his life chasing women, and he now had the contained, half-watchful air of a man who carefully hoards his energies. He opened his cabin door, prepared to lie down for an hour, but a young woman in a cool white sheath was combing her long, bluish black hair out in front of a mirror. When she saw George she turned, the comb still in her hand. He remembered the scene later—like a little shadow play, almost without words. He phoned the steward, and while they waited for the mistake to be straightened out, he took her down to have a drink in the first lounge he could find.

She was charming, sweet, and shy, so shy that he could

hardly get her to talk, but at the same time she did not appear to be insecure or frightened of him. She seemed to be mantled in a removed, untroubled unawareness that reminded him of the kind of purity which only exists in children's literature.

When their drinks came—the ship's specialty, something strong and dark and probably vicious under the various pieces of fruit—she brightened for a moment. She looked up at him for the first time, her eyes the color of half-opaque sea mist. "I *love* trying new drinks, don't you? I'm always curious to see what they'll come up with next."

George smiled. He realized that she probably had lots of little things to say along this line, like every woman. He would let her go on until she was enumerating the countless reasons why she couldn't sleep with him. He would listen quietly, without arguing, and when she was through, he would finally ransack her with great tenderness.

The steward entered the lounge with her hand luggage. He stood at the door, unable to focus in the dimness.

"Oh," she said, "there he is now. They've located my room. I'm so sorry if I put you out, but I could have *sworn* I was in the right place."

George rose to signal the steward, but she was already on her feet, crossing the room. He followed, but the headwaiter sprang forward with the bill, and when George got that cleared the girl and the steward were gone. He couldn't find them anywhere on the empty deck in the mist.

TRISTAN

George woke in the gray light, feeling the smoothly rolling water beneath him. The day was cold, the air icy. He shaved, bathed, and dressed with great care before he went down to breakfast.

He was aware of the sea quiet in the dining room, a suspension which was reinforced with the occasional sound of a fork against a plate, or the subdued voices of the waiters as they moved among the tables.

"Do you have orange juice? I mean by this orange juice from oranges."

"Yes, sir."

"*Fresh?*"

"Yes, sir."

"All right, orange juice. Then scrambled eggs."

"Yes, sir."

"Do you have English muffins?"

"Yes, sir."

"When I came up, I couldn't get English muffins."

"We have them now, sir."

"I'll have English muffins, then—*if* they have not disappeared by the time you get back to that mysterious kitchen of yours. Very lightly toasted, please. And then perhaps a coarse, very bitter marmalade. Will you faithfully promise me a very coarse, very bitter marmalade?"

"Yes, sir. Would you like your coffee now?"

"Coffee? I don't remember mentioning coffee? Have you put coffee down anywhere on that pad?"

"No, sir."

"But, do you know, I believe I'll have a cold glass of milk."

71

George went back to his cabin after breakfast. He lit a cigarette and dialed for the steward. A stranger appeared.

"I'm looking for the uniformed official who was on duty last night," George said, "during the boarding hours."

"I was on then, sir."

"Do you remember me? Do you remember the mix-up?"

"No, sir."

"All right, now look: We're going to begin from the very beginning. We're going to take things one step at a time. So you think we might try? Do you think it's worth a chance?"

"Yes, sir."

"All right. *Somebody* put a young woman in here by mistake, during the usual boarding confusion, during your usual chaos, during your usual hours of madness, and when I rang for the steward, I got one—one came, all right, as unlikely as this may seem—and he changed her room. He presumably put her where she originally belonged. Have you followed me so far?"

"Yes, sir."

"Fine. Who was this? Who would the steward be?"

"I don't know, sir. There must be some—"

"Confusion?"

"Yes, sir."

"Then do you think that you might unconfuse the confusion, and, by making a few reasonable inquiries, or perhaps by a great dint of official effort, *find out* just who the steward was?"

TRISTAN

"I can try, sir."

"Well, would you do that? Would you like to put all your many resources together and try that? Because if we can *find* the steward, he might just *possibly* remember where he has put the girl this time. He might just possibly remember where he has most recently mislaid her."

"Yes, sir."

"Because if the captain can dispense with your services for awhile, if the captain can let someone else actually *steer the ship*, we *might* get a little old-fashioned stewarding in."

The day stayed bad. The sky grew dimmer in the early afternoon. The moon stayed weirdly visible, more concrete than the faded sun, and by two o'clock the ship's lights were on.

George searched for the girl among the lounges and the bars.

"Which is worse on the heart, would you say, coffee or liquor?" he asked the bartender.

The middle-aged bartender was in a short red jacket with brass buttons. He looked Italian or French or Jewish. He had a receding hairline which emphasized his beautifully shaped, suntanned skull. He was polishing glasses. He shrugged.

"Well? Go ahead, guess."

"Liquor. I'm no doctor, though."

"Wrong. It's coffee. Interestingly enough, it's coffee."

The bartender shrugged again.

"You're going to do yourself out of a lot of business. I know a lot of men walking around with hearts."

"I don't make the profits. I just wear the red jacket."

"I went up to the States for a physical. A complete checkup. It cost me a hundred dollars. The first one I've had in—oh—must be fifteen years. I felt fine, too. I felt great. But I went up there for a physical, went a thousand miles over water, to find out that I have a heart condition. And what am I to think about that? Do you know what I wonder? Do you know what I wonder right now?"

"No," the bartender said, "I can't guess."

"Well, I wonder if I would have *had* a heart condition if I *hadn't been told* about it."

"Sir?"

"I wonder if I would have *had* a heart condition if I *hadn't been* told about it. Because it's the old tree-falling-in-the-forest argument again, isn't it?"

The bartender was putting the glasses away on a shelf. "You need good medical advice for these things," he said.

George paused in the doorway of a recreation lounge where two middle-aged couples were playing cards. They were wearing cruise clothes, but the women had thrown woolen sweaters across their shoulders, the sweater arms dangling at their sides. They sat with their arms crossed, their cards in their hands lying fanned out face down against their elbows.

"I promised while we were down there to buy Margaret one of those *lovely* Guatemalan skirts."

TRISTAN

"We're not going to Guatemala, Mother. We aren't even heading in that direction."

The woman was looking at her cards. "*I'm* not going to step into one of those skirts, of course, but you know my Margaret—just bone. She's nothing *but* bone, poor dear."

"It's your bid, Mother."

The woman looked over her cards, into space. "Oh, I don't know. Should I? Oh, well, for goodness sakes, no, I guess not, not with this hand. All right, yes. Pass . . . I'll pass," she said. "Isn't it cold, though? Isn't it *nasty?* Why, it's warmer home, down by us."

The waiter was standing at George's cabin door with a tray of bottles.

"Come in, come in!" George shouted. "I invented this drink. I take great pride in it, and I want to show you how it's put together. I call it Decline and Fall. Put the tray down over there, will you? Now watch. I want you to watch this very carefully. We use one part Spanish cider, one part Spanish brandy, one part crème de cacao, one part rum. Always use this Haitian brand. Don't think it will be the same drink without it—not Decline and Fall. Oh, yes, crushed ice. I wouldn't want you to try serving it without crushed ice."

The waiter looked at the performance with a dubious air. "Very tempting, very tasty, I'm sure, sir," he said.

"Well, you won't know until you try it. *Try* it!"

"Oh, I can't."

"*Can't?*"

"I'm on duty, sir."

"All right, all right, all right, *out* of here! Back to work. Man the helm. Stride the deck. Box the compass. Shoot the sun. Full steam ahead. Keep us on an even course!"

When the waiter had shut the door, George poured the mess down the sink.

The next morning, the second out, the air was warmer; by early afternoon the sun was pretty strong—hardly cruise weather yet, but the passengers appeared from their lairs and holes, stood around in groups on deck, cluttered up the stairs, and filled the shuffleboard courts—old ladies dangerous with sticks.

George wandered around through the activity looking for the girl. He narrowly skirted the hearts of things, the centers of energy. Social directors with whistles around their necks were briskly distributing mimeographed lists, forming groups, calling out names.

"Now listen, everybody, *please*," a director was saying. "Now listen, everybody, *please*, may I have your attention!"

George almost collided with a woman who was carrying a shuffleboard stick. She had short, darkish red hair and a big, puffy, freckled face. She was probably in her thirties or even possibly early forties. She was wearing one of those mannish, bulky slack suits that had first appeared after World War II and were now briefly back. However, George was staring at her eyes—the color of half-opaque sea mist.

TRISTAN

The woman held her shuffleboard stick out awkwardly toward George. "I've got this insurance around here," she said. "I found out that they'll leave you alone if you check out the sporting equipment; they won't try to find a *group* for you if you look busy. On the last cruise I checked out a shuffleboard stick every morning and then parked it beside me in a bar some place."

"Ah, I see," George said, still looking at her eyes.

"Well, what about it? What about finding a bar?"

"Sorry. I have to find someone."

George could not get away from her. He ran into the woman several times in the afternoon, while he was looking for the girl. The woman smiled in his direction, from the other side of a group, and held up her shuffleboard stick. George waved back and changed course. He found her later in the dining room, eating alone, but she did not look up this time, and he left as soon as he had finished his dinner. He ran into her in the bar that evening, sitting alone with the shuffleboard stick beside her. She moved the stick over and beckoned to him. He couldn't find an empty place anywhere else, and while he later remembered drinking with her in the bar, he did not remember when they had decided to go back to his cabin.

"I'm a teacher," she said, looking at George's bed, "that is, if I have to *tell* anyone. It's all over me, isn't it—the teaching game?"

George had had his share of oddball barflies. He lit a cigarette and rang for drinks while she went on talking.

"I'm one of those aging, slightly nonvirginal bachelor-girl types who go on tours looking for something, looking for almost anything, but you know what we wind up with, don't you? We wind up coming back loaded down with little sea horses in plastic paperweights, imitation shrunken heads with real hair, shells painted with scenes of foreign places, blowfish with light bulbs inside . . ."

"I'm half in love with somebody," George said, looking at her eyes. "Isn't that funny? Isn't that pretty funny? I've been married three times; I've got children scattered around in good schools from coast to coast; but I'm half in love with a girl I met just once, for a few seconds. I don't even know her name. Why, do you know, I don't even know what she looks like undressed. I must have drunk a fatal potion because I haven't felt the same since. I haven't felt at all well . . ."

"Confidences, confidences," she said, unbuttoning, "but we live, after all, in very personal times, very personal times."

George was unexpectedly pleased when he saw her without the slack suit, just before she doused the lamp. He realized now that nobody could have been *built* like the suit, and he found comfort where he found comfort, anyway, any way.

He was working on bits and pieces when the waiter knocked with their drinks. "Get back to the bridge," George shouted through the door. "Get back to the bridge and man the helm before we all go down!"

He woke in the middle of the night feeling cold. He tore at the edges of the covers several times, trying to get

TRISTAN

arranged right, but even under the covers his bones felt cold, as if his body heat were steadily dropping.

Then the moon cast a queer light, misshaping things. The woman was up, getting dressed, getting ready to go back to her cabin. He looked at the haggish, weary face, the hair skimpy and thin, the parted mouth, which, in the moon shadow, looked as if it did not have teeth. He shut his eyes quickly, and when he opened them again she was gone.

George woke late the next morning, on the third day. He felt less real than the water trembling in the glass beside his bed, the movement of the sea, the unexpected warmth, the laughter overhead on deck, the heavy, rotating spindles in the hold, the steady, weighty, ineluctable course of the ship.

He wasn't a deeply reflective man, but he was sometimes subject to strong moods like underwater currents, and since he had fought sadness, lassitude, melancholy, and despair before, he was not particularly worried.

"I have answers," he said.

He shaved with great care, chose an imported cologne, hesitated in front of his wardrobe. He could often change his mood according to what he wore, and since the old actor, the Tired Flesh, was about to stage a comeback, he chose a two-hundred-dollar sports jacket, a soft blue linen shirt, and a decidedly happy cravat.

He was looking forward to a good breakfast, but everything went wrong in the dining room, increasing his sense of loss and disorientation. When he arrived, nobody bothered to show him to his seat, but when he finally chose a table without help, a waiter was on him in a minute. "You can't sit there," he said, and ushered him instead to a table in the corner which was filled with dirty dishes, the remains of somebody else's breakfast.

George had to wait for half an hour before a surly busboy finally wandered over to clear away the mess. George decided to cheer him up. "You have a busy night at the helm?" he asked. "Did you keep us on course all right?" The boy looked at him darkly, without immediately answering, but as he turned away with the tray, he said, under his breath, "Screw you, Mac."

George still felt cold later up on deck. He felt the sun on his hands, the air's languid warmth, but he was cold. He sat back in a deck chair, threw a blanket across his legs, and closed his eyes, but he could not sleep. He opened his eyes from time to time to stare at the flickering water lights on the ceiling overhead. A bell rang somewhere, and then the silence again. He heard a door open and close behind him. He could not get comfortable. He decided that he needed a drink, and he descended the stairs, down one flight toward his favorite bar.

The dimness inside was comforting. The place was quiet, like church. Most of the passengers were up on deck, and the only sign of life here, besides the bartender, was the young couple behind him, toward his left—two pleasant-looking lesbians who were sharing a drink. They looked like twins; both bobbed heads blonde; and, in

TRISTAN

shorts, their legs were identically browned. George asked the bartender for a martini because gin usually warmed him first, and as he considered the strangeness and diversity of human love trying to assert itself against all odds, against all sense, he felt better—more alive.

A family group came next, charging through the swinging doors laughing and talking. The mother was big, florid, and fatty, and she was wearing one of those large, cartwheel-type picture-book hats that appear every other generation or so. She came in first, blindly, removed her sunglasses, and then turned to wave the others through, like a guide checking to see if the coast was clear. She had several other women in tow, friends or possibly relatives, and then last, the man and the boy. The man was not particularly small, but in that group he looked lost. He was awkwardly carrying a bakery box by the string. The boy was six or seven.

George moved down several barstools, closer to the lesbians' corner, to get away from the commotion. He tried his martini, and when he was satisfied that it was dry enough, that it was going to do, he put the glass down and looked in the mirror. He was straightening his cravat when he accidentally caught in the mirror the eye of one of the lesbians. He lowered his gaze and went back to his drink.

The family group got their drinks set up, and while these were being passed around, the mother was trying to light a birthday cake with a cigarette lighter. However, the lighter's slant was wrong; the flame soared without touching the candles, and the woman finally borrowed matches from the bartender. Then, while the candles were weakly burning, the group sang to the boy.

> Happy birthday to you,
> Happy birthday to you;
> Happy birth-day, dear Georg—ee,
> Happy birth-day to youuuu!

George looked in the mirror again, and when he saw the lesbian's face again knot into a frown he realized she was disapproving; he raised his brows and shrugged, a gesture meant to convey their mutual irritation. The lesbian jumped up, knocking her chair over backwards. "Hey, bartender," she yelled in a raucous voice, "do we have to put up with passes from this old fag?"

"Listen," the bartender said, evidently confusing George with someone else, "I've had all the trouble I want from you. I want you out of here—*now!*"

George was still looking in the mirror. He cleared his throat and straightened his cravat. Still not satisfied with it, he got off the barstool, and, everybody watching, he crossed the room and went through the swinging door. The voices started again when the door closed behind him.

He passed the swimming pool on the way back to his cabin. The area was cluttered with oiled, glistening bodies lying on beach blankets and on deck chairs, straw hats over the faces, the hands clasped across the stomachs, the feet up, showing blunt toes, the pale bottoms of the insteps exposed. The ship, heavy with this burden of sun bathers, cruised through the wrinkled, green water with an almost imperceptible motion.

TRISTAN

George felt a flash of pain across his chest. He stumbled, almost fell, and caught a rail. He held onto the warm rail for a moment, breathing with difficulty, and when his dizziness finally passed, he slowly made his way back to his cabin by keeping in the shade and avoiding the glare.

When he opened the door he saw the girl standing in the middle of his cabin, the girl with the eyes the color of half-opaque sea mist. She was wearing an open terry-cloth robe, but that was all. She was so heavily made up he hardly recognized her, and when she raised her arms, further parting the robe, he saw that her nipples were painted with a dark, red cakey substance.

"I *was* in the right cabin, after all, wasn't I, George? Isn't that funny? I was in the right cabin, after all."

George put his arms across his face to protect himself. "No!" he said. "No, please . . . ," but he fell down at the same time.

The Woman
in the Tree

Matthew Felder needed his little anxieties the way a heavy woman needs sweets. When one worry was gone, he was busy helping himself to another. He filed an application for a house in Willowbrook Estates, a suburban development set in rolling countryside, and, fully expecting complications, he went back home grumbling to himself. He did not discuss the possible complications with his wife, but when they were signing the closing papers with the bank several months later, they were both thinking the same thing: no complications, no trouble; notice?

"Ours," Matt said, leaving the bank, "is growing to be a humane age. Nobody's interested in old-fashioned shibboleths. Live and let live. Right? Still. The big question is now: Have we done the right thing? Do we want to live there?"

When he woke in the mornings in Willowbrook Estates, he would sense the house taking shape around him again, three levels closing in (counting the garage). Uneasy about this show of affluence, he believed that Irene must have made some colossal mistake in the household budget which had given them the *appearance* of being able to afford this place. He was half waiting for the bank to repossess. In that case, let them. He would be back where he belonged, in a five-room city flat.

As it was, the Felders were doing without extras. Matt was cutting the grass with an ancient hand mower. When they had moved in, the grass was almost a foot high, and he had to fight his way across it: getting little running starts, as if he were sneaking up, then attacking. He finally lost one of the handle bolts, and the handle sagged; the blades grew duller, and one wheel wobbled. To get the tough patches, he had to buy a sickle. The beefy next door neighbor mowed sitting on what resembled a motorized kiddy-kar, and, circling his house, he would watch Matt with his mower interestedly, as if Matt were some kind of nut.

Matt tried to speak when they were getting out of their cars after work, but the man hurried into his house, rolled paper tucked under his arm. At times, Matt felt that the man was secretly watching, wondering what he would do in the winter for an encore. The neighbor dressed like an executive: suits with narrow lapels and sincere, mediumly narrow ties, but he resembled a professional wrestler; rolls of meat circled his neck, and his watchful little eyes could have been searching for the vulnerable positions.

Perhaps, like Matt himself, the man didn't understand what the Felders were doing in a place like this. Matt wondered if he should go visit—barge in and talk it over. He could take Irene's budget with him, and they would sit down at the kitchen table over a beer. The wife would make pizza.

Then, in the early fall, the neighbors moved out quickly. A FOR SALE sign appeared on the front lawn beside the little white pole that held the cute lamp. As he got ready for bed and looked for his stomach medicine, Matt worried about the man.

"Bankrupt," Irene said, drawing her finger across her throat. "Wiped out. He got, against advice, a second mortgage, and when he couldn't make the payments, the whole empire went down over there, like dominoes."

Irene kept busy. She was with the Welcome Wagon Ladies, and greeted newcomers to the development with fresh supplies of calendars from the local mortuary and thermometers from the lumber company. Through Irene's activities, Matt got to know what went on.

"It was the fancy lawn mower with the upholstered seat, I bet," he suggested. "He would have been all right if he hadn't broken his back with that. I could have loaned him mine. We could have shared things and made it together."

He wished now that he had gone over with his budget and eaten pizza in their kitchen. He did not like passing the FOR SALE sign, which seemed to throw across the whole development a warning, a certain pall.

"The trouble with you is you aren't busy enough," his wife observed. "*Do* something with your spare time. Advance yourself."

THE WOMAN IN THE TREE

"I can't push thermometers."

"Who would take? Go back to school, have some of those courses they offer at night. The company pays for it. You should be a Shakespeare scholar before it makes you a vice-president."

Matt sampled, anxiously competitive. Unknown books had to be trapped and taken, like virgins. When the teacher mentioned a work, however offhandedly, Matt would quickly jot the title down. "I'll get *you*," he muttered, underlining with strong, swift strokes.

Matt was presently taking a survey of world literature under Professor Thomas Parker Berger. He felt as if he were in his element at last because he was attacking big, final literature like the Bhagavad-Gita and the Koran (with its explanatory translation by Mohammed Marmaduke Pickthall).

When someone asked Professor Berger what he was going to be teaching, he would lean back, and, in speculation, put his long, tapered fingers beside his nose. "Well, now, I don't really know," he'd say, smiling absently, considering a private joke. "I can't say yet. We'll have to wait and see, won't we, what the students have to offer?"

It was a classroom technique, a professional gimmick. On the first day, Berger would arrive before the students and, thrashing about in the empty room, push the teacher's desk back against the wall, remove the chairs from their comfortable security in their long rows until he had them in an awkward circle. Then he would leave and come back later and, as the chairs filled up, place himself somewhere in the circle, as if hiding. He fooled nobody, of course. Who else could he be?

"Well," he'd finally comment, "it doesn't look as if we're going to have a teacher, does it? In the meantime, I've come along to learn, so shall we start?"

Tired, hard-working people who had come to class after eight-to-five jobs studied him in silence, suspicious. They hadn't put their money down for this, but, faintly curious, they played along.

Taking the role, Berger paused after Matt's name. "Perhaps this term we can come to grips with the Old Testament," he suggested. Then he said something to Matt in Hebrew, but Matt looked at him blankly. Berger continued to fix him with his cold blue stare, pencil poised over the roll book.

Matt shifted in his chair. "Pardon?"

"Oh? Don't you know Hebrew? No? Pity. Well, we'll pass on."

Somebody else, Matt noted, got it in Greek.

University life wasn't what Matt had been anticipating. He had gone looking for contacts, dialogues, kindred spirits: a group drinking beer around a table after classes, perhaps some folk singing, but when the bell rang everybody hurried home. He finally saw the university as another Willowbrook; an investment maybe, a "development" no.

The house next door stayed vacant through the winter. The agent appeared one evening toward spring with a young, good-looking Negro couple. Matt was in the back

THE WOMAN IN THE TREE

thinking about his coming lawn problems when he saw the agent drive the couple right under the house into the garage—a swift, secret operation.

Matt marched over. The agent was standing with the couple in the drapeless picture window, and he could not ignore the bell. Matt barged in, hand out. "The name's Felder, next door. What can we bring over to make you people comfortable until you get yourselves settled in?"

The agent scowled, as if still anticipating trouble, as if this were some complicated kind of irony. The two prospects were taken aback, but, sensing Matt's predicament, the woman finally smiled. She gave Matt a shy, amused look. "Oh, we haven't made up our minds as yet, Mr. Felder. We are just looking around, as of this moment," she said.

A week later Irene came up to the bedroom with Matt's stomach medicine. "The Welcome Wagon Ladies are starting a petition."

"Against *what?*"

"What do you think? You need three guesses?"

"You get out of the Welcome Wagon racket immediately. Do you hear? I forbid you to go around with the Welcome Wagon people anymore."

"So I already said where they could go."

"When're they going to be working this block?"

"They don't tell me their big business now."

Matt stayed home from work, in wait, and on the third day, in the afternoon, he saw a car going from block to block. It was a bright, blowy Friday, and the wind kept

threatening the woman's hat. She ran up walks with her
head lowered, holding onto the hat brim with one hand.
Following her progress, Matt went from room to room,
peeking from the drapes.

Irene watched anxiously. "You don't know the woman,"
she said. "You don't know the woman at all. Be careful.
She may be a good woman. She may be a widow with six
kids. She's got troubles of her own. Be careful, please. We
have to live here."

"Live! You call this living? Go in the kitchen."

"Just don't answer the door. You don't have to answer
the door. She'll understand your feelings from out there."

"Go in the kitchen."

He waited, half crouched, beside the door. He saw the
woman come up the walk, her eyes, for some reason, on
the upstairs, and an odd expression crossed her face. Then
she backtracked to her car. Matt went outside. Irene was
in the upstairs window, still waving a handkerchief, like
Barbara Fritchie.

Matt went to the meeting. Irene saw him to the door,
and, hands clasped behind his knees, begged him not to
go. He broke away and walked the five blocks in case the
mob later decided to attack his car, but the place was less
than half full, and no mob spirit reigned there.

The chairman was almost inaudible. He began by
pointing out that he had given up his bowling night and
henceforth could not be counted on. The half dozen
speakers from the floor alluded to "a pressing problem"
without naming it. They seemed glad to duck back down.
Two well-dressed adolescents finally stood up, like twins

THE WOMAN IN THE TREE

giving testimony in church. They offered to scatter some garbage around the grounds here and there.

Matt very slowly got to his feet. The muscles on his face ached. He felt like an old man, but once he was talking, he felt better. "I'm not mentioning the colored people at all with you bunch," he said. Then he began to shout. "No, no, I'm talking about me, a white man. Who—in this good century—has an idea to die for? The white man? Who is dying now, losing empires, losing souls, losing self-respect, losing self-sustaining juices? White men. White men all over. No, go get up another petition. Get up a petition to save the white man before it's too late!"

A confused communication. By the end of it, people were nodding sagely, in agreement, as if Matt were on their side. But the meeting was over with nothing done. People were moving down the aisles. The chairman, who felt obliged to hear Matt through, was already putting on his coat.

The Negro couple moved in next door. He was a big man who wore executive-type suits and came home at night with a rolled paper tucked under his arm. He drove a big power mower which pulled around such attachments as a little red wagon, a seeder, a snowplow. He nodded toward Matt when getting out of the car, but when Matt was coming around the house with his broken-down mower, he politely looked the other way.

Matt could have afforded small payments on a cheap power mower now, but he had worked himself up into a state over his junky equipment. He was defying his neighbor with it.

The woman seemed friendlier. She had a small, childlike figure and a soft, fragile face. She spent a lot of time alone. Matt thought that his wife should go visit.

"Have a coffee *klutch*," he suggested.

"*Two* of us?"

"So a cult has to start somewhere."

"My mornings are full," she said. She was back with the Welcome Wagon bunch again.

"Well, take her a nice thermometer."

"She isn't on my beat."

The block finally decided that the new family wasn't different from anyone else. People began to ignore them, as they ignored each other.

However, Matt had discovered that the young couple was not perfect. They were terrible fighters. The fighting would start like clockwork on weekend evenings and go on into the small hours. They were as discreet about it as they could be. When they got raucous, windows banged shut, lights went out, but Matt, lying beside Irene in the dark, was haunted by images of mayhem. However, each appeared the next day apparently unscathed.

"It's a shame," he said, "young people fighting like that."

"Where would the old get the energy?"

Bringing the paper in one Saturday morning after a particularly bad night, Matt saw the woman up in a tree on their front lawn. She was wearing a long apricot-colored negligee, but she did not look so young now in the chilly gray light. She looked swollen and tired, a badgered human. Matt was both embarrassed and confused, as if he had been caught doing something wrong. He ducked back into the house.

"The woman next door is in a tree out there."

"What? Are you crazy? It can't be."

"So go have a look yourself."

"And appear nosey?"

"Then huddle in the house."

Irene went out to get the milk from the front stoop. "My God," she said, skittering back inside.

Matt thought about his broken-down hand mower. He felt a flicker of triumph for a moment. Who was the nut now? But, in truth, he felt sorry for his neighbor. Now they would visit each other's houses, and while Matt produced Irene's budget, the man would tell him how his wife's psychoanalysis was progressing.

Matt went to the phone upstairs. He cleared his throat and called. "This is your neighbor next door, on the right. I have something to mention of some delicacy. I happen to know where you can locate your good wife."

"My *wife?*"

"Try the tree," Matt said helplessly, "on your front lawn."

"Listen," the man said, "there are laws to protect citizens from drunks." Then he hung up.

Matt was afraid to go to the window immediately. He waited for perhaps ten minutes, and when he glanced out, the woman was gone. He did not know if the husband had gotten her out, or if she had finally climbed down herself.

Matt and the neighbor didn't nod anymore when they got out of their cars, and, toward the end of that summer, Matt treated himself to a cheap power mower in a Chicago discount store.

THE WOMAN IN THE TREE

Carolyn

De-De. De-De Van Dine. That is not her real name. We are new in this neck of the woods, having moved in only five years ago, and I called her that.

In the old days, before I broke my leg in several places, I could have at least checked the mailbox for the family name. They have over there for a mailbox a very cute idea. A little covered wagon complete with wheels that really turn. The wagon sits up there on its stilt, stuffed with *Reader's Digest* on Reader's Digest day and *Good Housekeeping* on Good Housekeeping day.

In any case, I never thought of looking for the family name on the side of the wagon when I could get about, and, anyway, I do not know why I cannot call her what I want. I take certain prerogatives as a sick man. As I have already said, I have broken my leg. As I have already said, we are going to call her De-De Van Dine. Ah, the dreams that I have about that girl!

That summer—the summer I'm talking about—I spent on the patio with my leg in a cast waiting for De-De to come out with the garbage. She has no brothers or sisters, and, although they have a hefty black maid, she has her little chores, these tasks like carrying out the garbage and mowing the grass. We are going to get to the lawn mower later. We'll save that. I don't want to rush things. Right now she's on garbage detail.

She has two costumes, or quick changes: denims cut above the knees for formal wear, and a green terry-cloth bikini, the bottom part a diaper that barely wraps around, fastened in the front with two huge pearl buttons just below the hipbones—buttons that sometimes study me, like eyes. Now De-De is small. The little legs are so perfectly wrought you're really amazed when she moves and you find out they're real—useful. But those wonderful boobs, which point every which way. She walks as if the rest of her has been carefully assembled or put together to support the bosom—the whole a clever piece of machinery, which, in the sun, is more than a trick of light.

But back to the garbage. De-De is of course carrying out the indisposable parts that the disposal unit will not take: tin cans, bottles, old razor blades, and, for some reason (a puzzle), flowers. Won't a garbage disposal chew up week-old roses? I don't know. Theirs doesn't seem to. She carries these flowers out with the trash, one or two broken necks hanging limply over the top. What a thing to have hap-

CAROLYN

pen. If I were a finished flower, I would choose instead the quick work the garbage disposal makes. But then I'm like that.

This summer—the summer I'm talking about, before I broke my arm—I spent on the patio with my right leg in a cast, and when not particularly busy, I held court. I had friends up from Philadelphia, friends down from Vermont. I had social obligations. Friends, friends. Talk, talk. The drinks promptly at four, and, later, in the mauve, dreamy Connecticut twilight filled with the half-blurred forms of great trees, we with precision and scientific know-how craftily lowered the sun on another day without feeling much pain.

Here is an average enough lemony twilight: Marvin and Dick squat in the plastic patio chairs with beers between their knees watching with me what's going on next door. Plenty is.

She's riding around among the elms on her father's big red power mower. She's a sort of modern nymph, you see, in among the two-hundred-year-old trees, going around and around on that thing. What is she thinking? I would not presume to say. She looks preoccupied. She is getting the wide, smooth circles just right.

The wives are in town. We mind the kids. This summer the role is reversed. I mind the kids. Beth runs back and forth to town—if not exactly to work.

The kids—mine, Marvin's, Dick's—are out under our elms having a tiny tea party. *Cute?* They're drinking tepid Kool-Aid from tiny plastic cups and passing around on tiny plastic plates something which I cannot see, and you would never guess.

"Ah," Marvin says, watching, "maneuver the mower around a little more this way, will you, child?"

Dick sips his beer. "Youth," he says, meaning something much more specific.

"Why can't I have something like that to take back with me?"

"Where," Dick wants to know, "would you keep it?"

"A nice cool, dry place would be the bin in the cellar, down among the potatoes."

"I saw that movie, too."

You know how it goes. On and on. Men when they get together like this must enjoy that kind of talk so much because it makes specific the muddled, inner, backwater wish. It is, in a way, a kind of group therapy.

It passes as thought. I hardly notice us as persons—the boys on the patio in their floppy bermuda shorts drinking Schlitz. We're disembodied hurt. We're words floating around inside little balloons, like comic-strip balloons, weightless, free, a little lost, a little detached. Now and then, as if an accident, two balloons bump. This is, if not in the conventional sense, a communication.

Let me explain: The words themselves as far as content goes are really deliberately quite meaningless. What we can enjoy is their shape, as if it were De-De's. We are in among the words enjoying what Marshall McLuhan calls "in-depth participation" because we are not in among anything else. This is called "creating an experience." With

CAROLYN

words we create from the ghostly idea next door on the lawn mower something as close to the real as we can get. Inside this playground we swing on swings, slide down slides. I know what's going on. *I* have these dreams.

I have fairly respectable, fairly responsible dreams in which, as a family man, I do not want to see anyone hurt or put out. Everything is arranged, ordered, tidy, as in a work of art. My family has gone away for the summer, staying in the mountains or staying at the shore, whatever they want, whatever they want; De-De's dad has taken his wife on an extended business trip, sometimes Europe, sometimes South America, because he doesn't want to neglect his wife, either; and while everybody is happy in this bland, generalized atmosphere of fulfilled obligations, I mount De-De like Atilla Rome—sometimes her place, sometimes mine.

The odors of cut grass and machine oil reach the patio, and in the changing, plum-colored air De-De sits solidly in the saddle, bosom bouncing a bit, but the spine is ramrod straight, suggesting the innocent attention she gives to her job, and to all basic things like that. As I have said, I don't know what she's thinking, but I believe that the thoughts of youth are long, neat, chrome-plated thoughts. These are going on, worlds away, on the other side of the trees.

Marvin slumps languidly in his chair stroking his beer can, as if half asleep. A certain fresh depletion in his energies stirs him a bit. He tries to crease the beer can with one hand. Some of the old ardor is in it. He looks at the half-bent can happily. Many years ago when the world was young Marvin worked a supply sergeant's racket in the European Theater of Operations—a fit enough operator, I bet, but he has since run to hair. While he is getting thin on top, tufts of hair adorn his nostrils, encircle his neck, and grow along the inside edges of his ears—as if in middle age he is about to be smothered in his own hair. I see in this shaggy goat who wears his bermudas with a sad, perplexed air the other level—the minor TV executive for a small station in Philadelphia.

Marvin's wife, his second, likes golf. She has won several cups. On the course she calls just about everybody Charley, whether male or not. "I feel like this is going to be my big day, Charley," she says, playing through, and the day is; it usually is.

Dick (whose name *is* Dick, not Richard, another type) now looks dreamily across the way, as if perplexed by both space and the dying light. The mower just then comes around a tree at a perfect little angle, and, while vision is fading, he strains to see the bouncy parts, those breasts, such excess treasures, which strike us all as idiotically rich and wasteful.

"Let's go get her," he says, without moving, and nobody answers.

When I am alone, when I am reading on the patio in the late afternoon, the child sometimes stands on her border delivering scraps of pertinent information, like a foreign agent who has only a moment to spare before he has to shoot a rapid or climb an alp. She was in college, but presently isn't.

CAROLYN

"I got bombed out," she announces. "I got shot down."

Her language reminds me of the troubled history of her time—phrases which have of course reduced the age to camp, or pop.

I said once that she has two costumes. She has many, but I choose to absorb her in bits, to make her last. Take this scene, for instance: the short, tight miniskirt which must deliberately look shrunken (like those sodden rags which distraught housewives used to hold up in the sanforized advertisements back in the thirties or forties); the backs of the knees bare, where the tiny hinges work perfectly, miniature miracles; the round little bottom like a beach ball; the partly outlined ribs; the short, straight brown hair which curves once into a point across the cheek; the swift, sudden, already departing, wide-eyed glance that suggests absolute acquiescence and contains, behind it, such deep, many-leveled pools of blankness. Oh, she is as infinitely fragile and as factual as a telephone number.

I haven't forgotten the tea party. Just then a child says: "Daddy?" in the dusk, out there under the trees—a call which wants nothing much more specific than reassurance. Whose is it? "We're here," I say (wherever that is), and let it go at that, happy because they're happy out there, and such good kids . . .

De-De's snap judgments and quick answers (which really answer nothing) suggest insecurity. All right, insecurity. What can we do with that? Sometimes when she comes over in the evenings she is unusually quiet, and I know that she has a letter from her folks. I ask from where. It is sometimes Brazil, sometimes London. Aren't they happy? Oh, yes, sure, they're happy. Then what's wrong? What's the fuss? She is now sitting on the edge of the bed, her head to one side, and she shrugs her shoulders, like a little girl. I can not see her face in the half light. I take her chin in my hand, and turn her face toward mine. Well? This is, she says, looking at me. What is? What we're doing. What we're doing? During these scenes, these dreamy lapses, she is several different girls, and I have to deal with them as they come along. All right, okay, let's just talk. She doesn't say anything. Do you want to go home? No, please don't send me home. She is on these occasions curiously modest, curiously delicate. She allows me to make love to her; she *wants* me to make love to her, but she believes that everybody will be all right if she doesn't respond. She has a faraway look while everything's going on. She has little reservations. I have removed her bra, under the pullover, but she wants to keep the pullover on. Why? Because. Because why? Just because. I am gentle, tender. She suddenly rolls away from me. Oh, hell, she says, I'm such a bitch. No. Yes. I know I am. I'm such a bitch. Let's get a drink, then. No. Come here. Please? She crosses her arms, grabs the edges of the pullover, and rolls the shirt up, over her head, and when the face appears, it's changed. I have to make quick adjustments . . .

De-De is going around and around next door. She mows with singular concentration, hardly glancing up. She lives alone in that world of lawn and trees and fading light. Who is she? What does she want?

CAROLYN

De-De wants to be virginal. Eighteen-year-old girls have aspired to be virgins before the 1960s, of course, but they have meant by this high ideal a war with time and change —the warrior who will cleverly pit herself against flux by politely turning her back on it. However, this isn't what this girl wants. She wants to ride the moment. She wants to celebrate being itself by staying briefly untouched. (What else but purity do the little-girl legs suggest, those icy, innocent legs? The brown hair is so short and straight, the face looks nude.) De-De wants that second that flowers have before they're cut. She wants to be a modern girl; just in that split second, before she descends with the wave, when she's still wearing the mini outfit, the broad orange belt, the white boots, the shirt which she has started to pull over her head—yes, in this timeless and breathlessly clear moment when purity reaches its peak. She wants to be this *is.*

Right?

Blooey.

Dick uncarefully peels the wrapper from an expensive cigar. He points it away from him, squinting along the barrel. "Well," he says, "that saddle's getting a workout, anyway."

Marvin clears his throat. "Love, which rules the stars and planets, can also give a man an erection."

"Love?" Dick says, and his question (or the word, at any rate, another balloon) hangs in there.

I read somewhere (probably in McLuhan) that Thai dialogue is read through a loudspeaker by Thai actors concealed from the audience. Dick's word *love?* means nothing, like Marvin's words, but just *is*, like the trees, the grass, the girl, etc.

De-De met Beth, my wife, once. Our four-year-old girl strayed over while De-De was doing the lawn. De-De stopped the tractor, dismounted, and, taking her by the hand, brought her back to the patio.

"I'm nervous on that thing when children are around. But otherwise I like visits. She can come any other time."

It's queer—De-De and Beth together, when De-De and I have another dimension; it's like several transparent overlays: the moment, the present, the now, the apparently real; then these dreams through which I look, and beyond that (because De-De doesn't share them) this nothing . . .

I'll get to the scene in a minute, but I want to tell you about Beth's great-grandfather—the start of things in this country, and partly the reason why we have such a big house. He was a tough, spunky little Dutch Calvinist whose nerve centers, a complicated exchange, understood more about money than my nerves and my head ever will, or ever could.

He was apprenticed at twelve to a German bookbinder, where he slept in a loft over a two-man shop and kept the dawn-to-dusk hours most wage-earners knew back in the nineteenth century. He came to America when he was still in his early twenties, opened his own bindery in Hoboken, New Jersey, and slept in the shop; and when he later opened two branches, he was still keeping the dawn-to-dusk hours. He was finally buying up stocks, utilities, real estate, and when he retired he had three houses. When he

CAROLYN

retired, he couldn't stop, of course. Do you know what he did? He spent his remaining years painting his houses. He'd hurry from the house in the city to the house in the mountains to the house on the shore—paint, ladders, and brushes in the back of the truck. He painted his places over and over, just to keep busy, until the day he died. I can see him, in my mind's eye, in the last hours of his life, standing on a ladder with a brush in the air, trying to hurry the job while the light still holds.

"What," Dick asks, "do you suppose her real name is?"

"Rosemary?"

"Joyce? Paulette? Donna? Nancy? Mary? Linda?"

"Susan?"

"Pamela?"

"Lana? Martha? Joanne? Marcia? Penny? Deborah?"

"Daisy?"

"How about Holly?" Marvin suggests—the two of them busy filling the patio, until we have run out of chairs, and then even out of standing room. I can hardly think over the noise the girls make.

Beth, my wife, has several degrees—her first from a young woman's progressive school, the kind of place where you will find notes like "Oedipus loves Jocasta" turning up on the bathroom walls. She doesn't use her degrees in the normal way, by teaching, but uses them all the same, all the time. She wears a Phi Beta Kappa key, and when she loses that, she has a spare. She keeps up on everything—myth, literature, theology, anthropology, art, etc., and when she recently joined the local Lutheran church (the

L.C.A. Synod, because she likes the modern architecture) she really read the hell out of old Luther. She went straight through—not just the popular, everyday stuff like *An Open Letter to the Christian Nobility*, *The Babylonian Captivity of the Church*, and *The Freedom of a Christian*, but smack on through the works. The poor pastor has his hands full.

De-De is still talking to Beth. She pats the top of the child's head and releases her hand. "Be sure and have her come back to see me, won't you, when I'm not trying to steer that monster over there?"

Beth asks De-De about school. She doesn't really listen to De-De's answer because she's busy telling De-De about the many interesting schools she's attended, and about some of the interesting things which have happened to her in these halls. She tells her about the "Oedipus loves Jocasta" remark because she wants to see if she's above the girl's head yet, and, if not, she can push on up.

De-De carefully considers the play (which probably has not made much sense to her). She finally says: "Can that marriage be saved?"—which is undoubtedly an old joke, I'm sure, just by the way she delivers it.

De-De doesn't exactly converse, either. "I got shot down. I got bombed out." She delivers in this deadpan fashion smack to the guts these slogans.

Beth goes on talking. She is busy tucking a blanket around my legs, and fussing with other parts—something she seldom does; but have you ever watched a woman like Beth not watch a woman like De-De?

CAROLYN

De-De has on the ragged, cut-down, sliced-up, torn-sideways denims, and the big breasts, separately disciplined, nest in a bra inside the ratty-looking orange pullover. The thing that really makes this bosom so appealing is the small, plain, oval face where some of the baby fat still lingers around the cheekbones.

When De-De leaves the patio, Beth says, "Good-bye," without looking up.

"Well," I ask, hoping to irritate, "who is that?"

"Are you kidding me? *I've* heard you talking to her before."

The fact is, Beth still expects to compete. She isn't against noisy costume jewelry or a miniskirt, and while she speaks, she is staring at her long legs which are, as a matter of fact, better than the girl's, and, at thirty-three, Beth knows it. She smiles to herself—a kind of cruel look.

"Do you know how old she is?"

(Which means: Do I know how old *I* am?)

And we've had *that* out. We're in De-De's place, back in her room at the top of the house—the walls covered with posters, the shelves cluttered with records, not arranged, but in helter-skelter bunches. I am on the edge in this teen-age atmosphere—this cliché idea of what the young are like. She is sitting cross-legged on the floor, and I'm still lying on the bed, staring at her bare back. Are you kidding me? she says, half turning around, away from the portable record player. Do you *know* what boys *my* age are *like?* Do you have any idea at *all?*

Dick leans forward. He lights his cigar, and, between

107

puffs, tries to talk. "Wait a minute. Look. I think I see a mission of mercy—a regular neighbor-type gesture."

The kids—two little kids, one of them mine—are taking some refreshments over, the remains of the tea party. De-De stops the lawn mower and dismounts. Very seriously she accepts the tiny cup and plate, having dainty little sips.

"Oh, my, yes," she says, "really delicious. This is *really delicious,* isn't it?"

She suddenly looks down at the plate. She studies it for a minute. "Hey, wait a sec," she says, her voice changed, "just what *is* this?"

I can't hear the mumbled answers. The little forms shift around on uneasy feet.

De-De comes across, from her country into ours, and when she reaches the border, she waits a moment for the children to catch up. They scamper across the grass, wondering if this is still going to be a game, or whether something else.

She is standing in front of us on the patio, just at its rim, still holding out the tiny plastic plate.

Dick looks up. "Well, now, what do we have here?" he asks, as if he has not noticed her before, but he is a gentleman, and he is certainly willing to give her his attention. Well, why not? What's to lose? Right?

"Do you men realize what's for dinner?"

I ease myself up a little in the chair, favoring the cast.

"Well, for heaven's sake," Marvin says, having adjusted his language because she's there, "do you know what this looks like?"

CAROLYN

There the kids have been, under the trees, having a tea party with Beth's birth-control pills.

"Oh, my God," Dick says, turning to me, "and *you're* supposed to be baby-sitting!"

My four-year-old speaks up. "We didn't really *eat* them, Daddy. We were just pretending."

"*Pretending?* Where're the rest of them?"

She opens her fists and holds her arms up toward me, the elbows slightly bent, and pills in both palms.

"Are these *all* the pills?"

She nods.

"Are you *sure?*"

"Yes, Daddy."

Dick picks up his beer. "Where're the women, anyway? These kids should be in bed."

I like Dick's wife. Grace is a very intense person; she has always struck me as a lot younger than she really is. Her people are fundamentalists. Grace was an only child, pretty close to her mother, and partly because she was so close, she never went through an obvious stage of adolescent revolt. She still doesn't drink, and when she started to smoke, after she married, she put her cigarettes out whenever she saw her mother coming up the walk.

Well, one day she got to brooding about it. She was busy cleaning the house, Dick was home sick, and the kids were all underfoot. She suddenly turned off the vacuum cleaner, dressed the children, lit a cigarette, and marched across the street to her mother's place. Grace's mother came out of the kitchen drying her hands on her apron, and when she saw the cigarette, her face fell.

"I smoke now," Grace said. "I'm a wife, and a mother. I'm thirty years old; I have a lovely home of my own, and I smoke cigarettes."

Dick and Marvin squat down among the children, and, worried fathers, they supervise while the kids put every last pill back into the plastic container—the two men checking them against the little calender in there, another complete world, its tiny figures precise.

"Well," De-De says to me, "back to the old salt mines."

I suddenly have several thoughts which are so luminous and so bold that they take my breath away for a moment, and I have to sit back in the chair. I have just wondered why she has to live next door, why she has to come over here, or why, indeed, she has to *be* if she has nothing to do with me: and then I realize, in the same instant, that the house in which I live, the chair on which I sit, the beer which I consume, the grass which I cultivate, the trees which I love, the moist twilight air which I breathe have nothing to do with me, either. I realize that, like a final, indivisible element in a chemical solution, I am separated from everything around me—everything.

The children mill about us, and, picking up the empty beer cans, they have a new game worked out. They chase each other around our chairs. They're very tired, and they are beginning to get raucous. I ask them to hold it down, and while I am wondering what to do with them until the women get back, I hear the lawn mower starting again across the way, on the other side of the trees.

Dick's boy says: "Why can't we go over there? Why can't we watch Carolyn mow the grass?"

CAROLYN

He is standing next to me. I hear both the lawn mower and the name "Carolyn," and now, around the name, which I have, which has become mine, I can construct a new, another metaphysics.

Let me tell you a story . . .

The Diary of
a Short Visit

We left New York City by car late Sunday night and began the long drive up into New England in the midsummer heat. We practically had the north-bound traffic routes to ourselves. The New Jersey cliffs had a good deal of light without sound; the river was without cargo, and the city behind us, level upon level, was like a powerful motor that has stopped humming.

When we reached the Saw Mill River Parkway, the surrounding green cooled the air a little, and the half-obscured foliage, lit here and there by parkway lamps, hung with such sweetness in the dark that it permeated the car. I was suddenly so held by a sense of particularity that I could not remember any borrowed moment of happiness in my life that was as temporary and probably as deceptive as this. I am a demonstrative person, and if I had been with a woman, almost any woman, I would have told her that I loved her, but I didn't want to scare my young daughter, and I drove on thinking about the routes down to the shore and the two weeks together on the water. We had these two weeks together out of the year.

When we talked, we talked about what she was doing in school, what films she had seen, and what books she had read. I would ask a question, and she would answer, as if the information were going on file somewhere. Everything was terribly crystallized with mutual self-consciousness, each moment enunciated. Finding out whether she wanted to stop for a Coke, then buying, then drinking it, was grandly highlighted and weighty, and when done, done just so. With this astmosphere, she wasn't really she yet, I wasn't really I.

We were on the Post Road, just outside of Fairfield, when she finally volunteered her first piece of information. "Mother wants me to call her when we get in tonight," she said.

"Oh? Then you'd better call."

She didn't say anything else, but she was still looking at me.

"Right?"

She nodded. I could see the faint, very faint movement of her pony tail in the semidark. "Yes," she finally said.

She didn't know me yet. She was waiting. She had a little bit of her mother's sense of superiority in her that, in the mother, masked fear. I could feel it like a faint breath.

I was trying to explain where we were going and how we were going to spend the next two weeks. "This is just a beach, which isn't particularly impressive as beaches go. Don't be expecting Acapulco, Claire."

"Oh, I wasn't particularly impressed with Acapulco," she said.

There was no connection between the solid, boisterous four-year-old that I had once lived with and this slight, delicate girl who was just beginning to curve. Connections, connections . . .

The house stood a little apart from the other beach houses along the curved shore. In the dark the coming and going of the surf and the pungent sea smell was like the essence of the two weeks ahead. Florence Weikert, the agent, lived across the street. We went over together to pick up the keys. An electric guitar was whining inside, and, judging from the general noise, the place was alive with teenagers. I rang the bell several times before the racket finally ebbed a little.

The musician came to the door still holding his guitar. Jim Weikert was a short, sturdy-looking teenager with blond bangs, and, still wearing his trunks, he looked like a basic piece of engineering. I told him who we were.

"I'll have to get Mom," he said, looking at Claire. "She's lying down."

We unloaded the Mercedes in the dark. The house was huge and shadowy, filled with secret recesses, curious corners, and sudden briny smells. The little end-table lamps cast islands of light everywhere, enlarging the rooms, deepening the dusky places.

Claire called her mother to tell her we had arrived

THE DIARY OF A SHORT VISIT

safely. I went out on the screened porch, then down the steep steps to the beach to leave them alone together. While I was going down the steps, I heard Claire saying, "Yes, Mother. No. Yes, yes, yes. Oh, no. Yes, Mother . . ."

I slept late. The day was hot and hazy, the sky almost white. The tide was just coming in, and the sea was very still. Kids from the Weikert place were crossing the sand beside us to get down to the water. I could hear their voices from the bedroom. I walked out and stood in the porch doorway. Claire was lying in the porch swing reading *War and Peace.*

"I'm sorry I overslept. You should have called me."

She shook her head without looking up from her book. "Oh, that's all right, Daddy," she said, her mind on Tolstoy.

I watched the kids. The half-bare figures made me realize how far away I was from the city, and they were, on a city man, a little shock against the senses, as if I had suddenly turned a corner and come on them unaware. A tall girl in a backless white suit just about took my breath away. She reminded me of my current mistress, a young woman who would have been good for Claire. I had thought about bringing her with us, but I knew that if I had, my ex-wife would have been instantly in touch with her lawyer about the situation.

Flora Weikert's son was in the group. He was in the same trunks he had been wearing the night before, and his body was almost black from the sun. He looked into the porch and whistled, in a friendly way, but Claire did not look up. I wondered if she even believed he was whistling at her. And *that* was her mother all over again—terrible inferiorities that had produced, in the mother, the superwoman. How could I stop my child from going the same way? Toward all those poisons?

We went shopping later in the morning. I remember two things about that shopping trip. First, the way she looked: apprehensive and tense, as if she had her mind on something else. I found out that she was worried about getting back to the house because Teresa had said she was going to call. I decided that I was going to have to get in touch with my own attorney and see what I could do to get these calls stopped. I knew what Teresa was up to.

Second, I got my first real reaction from Claire while we were in the store. There was no supermarket anywhere near, and everything in the stuffy little grocery was, I guess, pretty expensive. In any case, I picked up four jars of asparagus and put them in the basket. I was wheeling the tall, old-fashioned narrow cart through the crowded aisles at the same time, and she suddenly put her hand over mine on the handle.

"Oh, *no*, Daddy," she said, "don't you dare! Not at that price."

I hadn't paid any attention to the price one way or the other. Curious, I picked up the jar to see. "That's high, is it?"

"Why, it's awful! It's outrageous."

"Do you *like* asparagus?"

"Oh, yes, but . . ."

THE DIARY OF A SHORT VISIT

"Okay. Then we'll damn well have asparagus."

What was interesting about all this is important: The mother once commented, when Claire was just two, that the world was such an evil place she sometimes thought about walking into the sea with her child in her arms. Now, given that view of things, Teresa had to be pretty merciless herself, and she was never amused or touched by anybody's minor foibles. I could remember Claire's dry remark about Acapulco as a standard way of handling everything—suspicious, alert, slightly above it, but on the way home from the grocery we played a little game. It was a game because it went on so long. Claire told me that I shouldn't be allowed to shop, and I called her a penny-pincher. The little insults brought us half close. She would study my face, laugh, and shake her head. I decided that I could use this friendly myth to advantage: the half-helpless, woolly-minded old dad who had to be carefully watched.

Teresa called after lunch, just as we were getting ready to go out on the beach. I was fixing a martini to take with me. Claire picked up the phone in the living room. There followed that yes-Mother-no-Mother routine again.

"Daddy?" she finally called. "Mother wants to speak to you a minute."

"*If* he can put the martini pitcher down that long," Teresa said to me.

"Claire's having a Coke."

"I would appreciate it if you saw she had something besides sugar in her system."

"I'm going to bring her back with a big appetite for

asparagus. Why don't you ever feed the child asparagus?"

"And women," Teresa said. "She doesn't have to be around your women, does she?"

"*What* women?"

"All right. I just wanted you to know that I'm waiting for one false move."

I had learned a long time ago to keep my temper with her by just saying, "Oh, go to hell, Teresa" in a quiet voice. I told her to go to hell and hung up.

Claire was in her bathing suit. She had cleaned up the kitchen, and now she was busy-busy emptying my ashtrays before we went out. She swung ashtrays out from under me at the sight of a single dead cigarette, which was, of course, one of her mother's habits again. I rubbed the side of my face.

"I'm sorry," I said. "I don't want to bother you with our fights."

She had her back to me. She was going into the kitchen and did not turn around. "I wasn't particularly listening," she said.

It rained the next day. Claire read. I got restless toward afternoon. I suggested that we find out what was going on in the village. There was only one movie house there, and we ended up seeing a rerun of *Bambi*. The moment of genius in that movie has to do with the father. Like Claire, I was also the product of divorced parents, and the moment in which the big muscled stag first appears on the bluff outlined against the sky always grips me, but the picture from then on ceases to hold my attention. I glanced

THE DIARY OF A SHORT VISIT

at Claire's small, pale, cameolike profile in the half dark, wanting to leave, but she appeared to be absorbed.

We stopped for sodas on the way home. We sat up in front of a high wooden soda fountain with a marble counter top. I watched Claire still working on her soda when I was through. She had abandoned the ponytail today, and her chestnut brown hair hung straight down her back.

"Claire, do you ever have dates? I don't mean serious courting, yet, of course, but do you get out with kids your own age?"

She briefly turned her face toward me without taking the straw from her mouth. Suspicious. "Oh, yes. Sometimes."

"What does 'sometimes' mean?"

She looked down at her soda. Then shrugged. "Oh, I don't know. Just 'sometimes.' Mother's very worried about sex," she said.

I didn't say anything else right away. I was wondering how to handle this. I finally paid the bill and held the door. "I'm not going to tell you, either, that some maternal worrying isn't normal, of course," I said on the way to the car. "But I want your living to be done with real people as well as the big characters in books. I know about literature, baby. I was a great reader once."

"What happened?"

"Oh, I don't know. What usually happens? Making money, I guess. What shall we eat tonight? Let's get a duck, some oranges, and some wine."

The weather cleared a bit, and we moved the dinner

119

table out onto the porch. While we were having our duck, the phone rang. Claire answered it. She came back onto the porch.

"It's for you, Daddy. It's Mrs. Weikert next door."

Flora inquired about the house, asked how we were getting along, and apologized about the weather. Then she wanted to know how I felt about her son taking my daughter to a beach party. "I thought it would be such a good opportunity for her to get to meet some nice young people around here," she said. "Jim will call her himself, of course, but I'm clearing the deck with you first."

"Well," I said, "the beach will be pretty wet, won't it?"

"Oh, but you know kids. They've been planning to go, and, short of a hurricane, they're going."

"Well, I don't know . . ." Claire said. She looked at me. "What do you think? Will you get along all right, Daddy?"

"Oh, yes, I think so. The beach, of course, will be wet."

Jim Weikert showed up in a sweater and tight khaki pants, but he seemed well behaved. He asked me when Claire ought to be back.

Claire looked at me. She was in jamaicas and a cotton pullover. I couldn't see young girls going on dates without a dress, but they were headed for the beach, and I finally said nothing about her clothes. "I don't know," I said. I was so new to all this. "What time does your mother usually want you in?"

"Oh. Around eleven. Usually."

"Okay. Twelve, then. But no later."

THE DIARY OF A SHORT VISIT

As soon as Claire left the house, I phoned my attorney at home about Teresa's calls. I couldn't get much satisfaction. He said that he would get in touch with her attorney in the morning and try to get the calls limited and put on a schedule so the girl wouldn't feel she had to stay close to the house all the time. I said that I didn't want Teresa calling at all, but he said he wasn't sure that could be arranged, short of having the phone removed. I knew that if I removed it, I would have Teresa at the back door.

I lay down on the couch with Tolstoy, but I fell asleep, and when I woke it was after one. I didn't stop to call Flora. I charged over there, but she was out, and the house was dark.

I was already close to panic. I couldn't stay in. I got out the Mercedes and drove slowly through the village, but it was empty, and I went out along the network of shore roads. I knew the search was pretty useless because I could not possibly track down every side-by-way where that little bastard could have parked.

It started to rain again. It was soon driving against the windshield with great force. I had difficulty maneuvering. The trip was like a dream without sound. Enclosed in the rain, within the smooth, cold silence of the car, I was beginning to talk to myself. I stopped several times to call the house. I watched the hands on my watch move from two to 2:30, then 2:45.

I finally went back into town and stopped at the police station. It was filled with wet, disheveled, milling adolescents. Everybody was talking at once. The police were still trying to sort them out and get addresses. I saw the Wei-kert boy first. He was sitting on a bench with his head bandaged, his guitar beside him. Claire had gone back to the rest room, and I was already shouting at him when she came back.

I wasn't making much sense. "Is your guitar all right?" I yelled. "Is it okay? Did you damage your instrument?"

He narrowed his eyes at me and moved the guitar closer to him. "Take it easy," he said. "Just take it easy, will you?"

"Where's Claire? *Where's my daughter?*"

A cop stepped between us. He wanted to know who I was.

I didn't answer. I saw Claire out of the corner of my eye, and I turned around to find out if she was hurt, but I was still shouting at the boy. "Oh, why don't you go jam a plug up your ass and amplify your voice," I suggested.

The cop took my arm. "Now just a minute," he said.

Claire wasn't injured. She looked wet and flushed but otherwise all right. "Oh, *Daddy*," she said, "it isn't his fault. Our group was *raided* by some other kids. Can you imagine? What we've *been* through?"

"We've been trying to call the house for hours," the cop said.

Claire nodded. "Oh, Daddy, they finally called Mother in New York."

We drove back to the house through the heavy rain. I called Teresa as soon as we arrived, but she didn't answer. We both knew where she was, but we didn't mention it. We didn't mention her at all.

THE DIARY OF A SHORT VISIT

Claire took a hot bath, piled her hair on top of her head, and put on my bulky robe. She still had a flushed look, a heightened color, and I gave her some tea laced with rum.

"Oh, God," she said, dramatically, "what a night!"

I smiled at her. "Drink your rummy tea," I said.

She was still too thrilled about it to settle down, and she called Jim Weikert. They spent a half hour going through all the events of the evening again. She spoke to him in that solemn, deadly important-sounding voice adolescents use with each other over everything. They'd had the evening of their lives.

Claire was generally changed. I do not know how to put it. Happier? She was more sure of herself. A specific person. She had come through a minor emergency with flying colors, and she had found out something about herself. She realized that she could become an adult after all. She knew she had a lot of time to make up. We finished the cold duck and sat talking. We had so much to say. The rain was still falling, and because of the storm we didn't notice that the night was gradually lessening.

I saw the car lights first. She pulled up into the drive behind the house. Claire looked at me. "Yes, Claire. Now we go forth to face the conscience of the race."

When I saw Teresa's face, I knew that Claire was not going to be able to hold out. She was going to have to go with her. "God knows, you must have worn the rubber clean off the wheels getting up here, Teresa," I said, but she didn't answer. She wasn't speaking to me at all.

"Claire," she began, "my child, my baby, my infant . . ."

When Claire was dressed and packed, she stopped beside me for a minute. She put her hands out. "I don't want to say goodbye, Daddy," she said.

"I wish you wouldn't leave in this rain."

"I'm waiting, Claire," Teresa said.

"We'll go somewhere farther next year. Maybe fly to Europe."

Teresa picked up Claire's suitcase. "We'll see about that," she said.

"Oh, go to hell, Teresa," I said.

When they were gone, I sat down with a drink. I could not sleep. Claire had left her book, and I read Tolstoy for an hour or so without knowing what I was doing. I could have been reading Russian. When it was lighter I went out for a long walk on the beach.

The daylight came slowly, what light there was, and the storm finally subsided in northern Connecticut, but the heavy rain was moving southward along the coast, and Teresa and Claire never reached the end of it. Teresa tried to pass a Volkswagen camper on a long, swerving curve going up a slippery ramp. In that curtain of rain the mother may have been thinking she was going into the sea at last with her child beside her, but I will never know what, if anything, Claire was thinking about.

THE DIARY OF A SHORT VISIT

The Madame Bovary Complex

The last time I went home I stopped in Grand Central to call first. I had not told anyone I was coming, and I wanted to be sure that they met me with the car. My mother's voice on the phone sounded characteristically unsurprised, but happy. "Oh, yes," she said, "just tell us the time. We'll get you. We'll be glad to pick you up. How are Catherine and the children?"

"They're fine, Mother. They aren't with me, though."

"Oh? Why? Where are they?"

"Now don't worry. Catherine had to get some work done. She went up to the lake to do it, and she took the kids with her."

"Well, we'll be waiting for you. We'll be there. It's good to hear your voice."

"It's good to hear yours, Mother."

The New York, New Haven, and Hartford took a little

over an hour. The warmth outside the air-conditioned car looked cindery and corrosive. The sun looked close to the ground. The late fall light seemed to be coming from within the bushes and the tall, leaning weeds along the track. The gray frame houses with washing in the back-yards had bleak, reflectionless windows. We zipped past Stamford, Norwalk, and Westport, the railway station posters advertising Radio City Music Hall, Leonard Bernstein, and Miller's High Life.

When we were just outside Bridgeport my nervousness increased. I went through an inexplicable seizure of inertia. I couldn't swallow easily, and I couldn't lift my hands without effort, but I went through this every time I came home. As we move back towards childhood and young adulthood, we approach the center of the unanalyzed life, where the residue from every ancient emotion seems coarse and sluggish, where old griefs, humiliations and guilts lie undisturbed at the bottom of things, like great blind fish in hibernation . . .

I was home from college that summer. I usually visited friends on the West Coast or walked around Europe during the months of July and August, and I was restless as soon as I stepped onto my parents' front porch. I was looking for something to occupy my time. I was through for the summer, at least with reading.

Now the Woolgroves—the original Woolgrove family —were my parents' friends. The Woolgrove names on the local headstones went back to the early seventeen hundreds, and the Woolgrove money was everywhere. Dwight Woolgrove purchased the place next door when he got married the previous winter, while I was away. Dwight was in his thirties, over ten years my senior, but there are some men who seem to hold the stamp of the child about them all their lives, so that the boy stands forth in the man even when he is making thirty thousand a year. In Dwight's case, it was a large, generous bumptiousness, and from whatever angle you chose to observe his wife, you could not have seen her as exactly passionate about him. Dwight was a big boy with sloping shoulders and heavy hams. When he got home from New York at night he immediately made himself a drink and without removing dress shoes and socks climbed into the large, loose, floppy shorts that did nothing for his behind, but the Woolgroves had helped to settle the town, and he was a Yale man, and he had that calm, authoritative look of most Yale men. He had a fundamental sense of the basic pleasures, and it was half disarming to watch him relax in the evening. When he was fresh from the shower, all curried and combed, he'd sink back with a sigh into the lawn chair under his favorite elm. "Oh, it's so *good*," he'd say, "to be a hundred miles from the nearest Jew. Lela, be a good sport, will you, and put just a little more whiskey in this water?"

My mother in her New England way found out as much about the new bride as she could. Lela wasn't from New England. She had come from Altoona, Pennsylvania. She was about my age. Dwight had interrupted her education, but she still painted a little, and she liked to read. Dwight

127

was away a lot, and my mother—my good mother—
thought it would be nice if I took her over some of my
books.

Dwight was home the first day I went. There were times,
of course, when Dwight appeared to be fifty or more. This
was the New England in him, and it happened whenever
he was talking about his neighbors and their families.

"You're Ethel Myers's only grandson, aren't you, son?
My God, when I first saw you in your front yard, I thought
I'd seen a ghost," he said, as if he'd been my grand-
mother's contemporary. "Something about the eyes and
nose. Where is the good woman resting? I don't seem to
recall."

He spoke in a booming voice. He reminded me of my
uncles, who were older, and although—or because—I
knew he was such a bore, I was quite shy around him. "She
isn't," I said. "She's in California."

Lela Woolgrove came into the room just then, looking
very breathless, and we stood up. "The dog's loose," she
said. "She broke her rope. I think she's heading for the Eddelson's garden again."

Dwight put his cigar down. "Oh, hell, just a sec, will
you, Dick?" he asked, as if I had come to see him.

Then he was gone, out the front door, and we heard the
car leave the drive. That was the first impression Lela and
I ever shared together—Dwight's heavy car crunching
gravel.

"Dwight *won't* get a chain," she said, "and that setter
goes through every rope he buys. I think it's *such* a shame

THE MADAME BOVARY COMPLEX

a big dog like that can't be loose. Why, I'd never heard of such a law."

I had never seen Lela up close before. She sat on a chair upholstered with needlework, a cockatoo surrounded by an exotic collection of flowers and loose leaves. She was big and beautifully made. She had just come from the tub, and her skin still looked faintly flushed. There was a glimmer of bathroom sweat above her upper lip. Her full upper lip stood out just a bit, giving her mouth an opulent, sensual look, like a hard, immature apricot. Her long black hair was pulled away from her slender face and tied in a bun in back. She was wearing a cool-looking broomstick skirt and a sleeveless yellow blouse ornamented around the collar with tiny green buds. She had imported leather sandals on her strong feet and a silver chain around her left ankle. Her arms and legs were smooth, brown, and bare.

However, my mother's hopeful dossier turned out to be misleading. The "painting" she had spoken about was a bad realistic still life: oranges, pears, and candles set against a mud-colored drape, carefully and painfully "rendered," as they say, as if Cézanne had never existed. The "college" was a private two-year Christian institution for young women set in the farmlands of western Pennsylvania, one of those places which stresses personal maturity for the Christian homemaker in the modern world, and where a course in the development of the novel still included works like *Ivanhoe* and *Silas Marner*, and, for the contemporary pitch, *The Robe*.

I got so wrought up about this—a mixture of amusement and anger—that for a moment I could not speak, and my eyes filled with tears. Then I said: "Oh, my God, Lela, did you actually *pay* to get in this place?"

She could have gotten miffed about this attack on her old alma mater, but she was a sport. She took it very well. She was, in fact, vaguely helpless, always conciliatory, as if she were half willing to assist in her own destruction, which from the beginning made her seem so charming. She smiled. "I guess I was being Christianized, wasn't I?"

"I guess you were, if that's the word. Look. Can you get me a piece of paper? Can you find a pen?"

She located a bridge scorepad and a tiny tasseled pencil. "Will these do?"

"I guess. Now. Have you read James Joyce?"

She was a little bit embarrassed by this time. She felt the pressure. She thought for a minute, as if she were actually wondering. She bit her lip. "No," she said finally, "I guess I haven't."

I wrote the names of Joyce's three novels down on the pad, then thought for a minute and added *Dubliners.* "Henry James?"

She bit her lip again. "Let me see. Now don't tell me . . . Did he write *Daisy Miller?*"

"A flimsy bit. A short story, really. What else?"

"Of Henry James?"

"Yes."

She shook her head. "I don't know," she said.

"Well, we'd better begin with *The Ambassadors,* I guess. What about Marcel Proust?"

THE MADAME BOVARY COMPLEX

"No. No, I don't *think* so."

"By the way. Do you read French?"

"No."

"All right. I have À *la recherche du temps perdu* in translation, boxed and waiting. *That* will keep you busy. How about Aldous Huxley?"

"No."

"We'd better start with *Point Counter Point*. This is not organized, of course. I'm just jotting things down as they occur to me. What about D. H. Lawrence? I'm sure the good institution didn't let you get into *Sons and Lovers*, did it?"

When I was through—there was no real stopping place, but I had used up the scrappy scorepad—I handed her the list. She folded the tiny slips of paper and put them away in her big purse, as if she were secreting somewhere in there among the Kleenex and the makeup equipment a small wad of precious bills. The gesture—such an epiphany of trust—laid me low.

Dwight came back with the setter, a big unruly bitch that bounced across the front parlor and finally ended up getting half of herself into my lap. Her hot, heavy forepaws dug into my thighs for support, and her tongue dropped saliva on my hand. Dwight got us disentangled at last and herded her through the house toward the back door. "You're a naughty, naughty girl," I heard him telling her, trying to tie her up again under the elm.

I went over the next day with an armload of books, but the part-time maid said that she had gone to the beach. I left the books with the maid, and went out to look for her.

A few cars were parked above, their tops just showing over the seawall, and a few mothers, fully clothed, were sitting among the rocks watching their kids, but it was a weekday, and on the whole the sand was deserted. There is a particular gray spatial arrangement that New England shores have in common—the sun usually behind a steady white haze, the isolated wheeling gull which sounds like a crow, the broken shells, the drying upturned horseshoe crabs, the froth and spit at the sea's edge, and the sand slightly darkened where the water hits it. Even the salt smell has an essentially lonely quality, and to come across that beautiful body lying against a backdrop like this was a little weird. She was like a figure of beneficence which allegorizes all the forces of love and idleness. She was shiny with oil. Her legs were darker than I remembered. They were almost black, and they made me wonder about the pale, milky white band of skin above which would resemble, in contrast, an area staked out like a target.

She was lying on her back, and when I spoke, she leaned forward a little on her elbows and took off her dark glasses. "Oh," she said, "hi! I have trouble seeing with all this guck I'm wearing. It gets on my glasses."

"You surely don't need oil. Your skin couldn't burn, not as dark as that skin is."

"Oh. This keeps me from drying out. I don't want to look like old leather."

I sat down beside her and pulled my T-shirt over my head. "Well, you don't. You look amazingly like an oiled sacrifice, though."

THE MADAME BOVARY COMPLEX

She didn't answer. She rummaged around among the paraphernalia in her beach bag until she'd located a can of Tucks. She placed the moistened pads against her eyelids, put the dark glasses back on, and lay down again. Then, still not settled, she raised her bottom an inch and tugged at the suit around her hips.

"Where did you meet Dwight, Lela?"

"In a Red Cross canteen in Spartanburg, South Carolina."

"And that's pretty far from Altoona, isn't it?"

"I was visiting my dad between semesters. He was working on the base. He had a civilian position. My mother and father are separated. My mother isn't—well—too well, and I used to stay with my dad a lot. What does the word paludal mean?"

"Paludal? It has something to do with marshy places, I guess. Why?"

"Use it in a sentence."

"Oh, I don't know. . . . That's a paludal region?"

"What's a paludal region?"

"A swampy place! I just used it in a sentence."

She nodded. She wasn't looking at me. She lay on her back talking straight upward. "That's right. Yes, that's very good. That's the word I looked up today. When Dwight's gone, and I don't have to hurry with breakfast, I look up a different word every morning over a cup of coffee. Then I use it in a sentence."

"That's very wise. Where has Dwight gone?"

"He's in Denver on business."

"A traveling company is coming to Bridgeport with *The*

Magic Flute. I don't know the company, but we just might take a chance and drive in. Yes, I think perhaps we had better see it."

"Oh, that would be nice," she said dreamily, but I wasn't convinced she realized she was being invited.

I turned carefully over on my side, my chin in my hand, my elbow dug painfully into the hard Connecticut sand. "I want to sleep with you, you know, Lela," I said.

She removed her dark glasses, took the Tucks from her eyes, sat up, looked at me for a minute in silence, and then began to pack her stuff.

"Well? *Will* you see the opera with me?"

"No."

"Why?"

"You know why," she said.

I went alone with my sullen pride to hear the opera. When I came back and put the family car away, I noticed a light on in the Woolgroves' living room. I crossed the lawn and knocked on the front door. The dog barked for a minute behind the house. Then Lela was standing in front of me. She was wearing red shorts, her hair was lying on her back, and she was holding my copy of *Ulysses* against her bosom.

"I saw *The Magic Flute,* anyway. I went alone."

"Oh, good. I'm glad. Did you like it?"

"Oh, yes. It was, after all, quite good."

She came out, still holding the book, her finger marking the place, and shut the door behind her. "I'll just get some air with you for a second. It's *such* a hot house. Was Bridgeport hot?"

THE MADAME BOVARY COMPLEX

We sat down together on the porch swing and stared at the weed-filled lot across the street. In the humid, close night a mist clung to the ground. The streetlight in front of our house next door lit the lower parts of the giant maple. A couple went by, about our age. "Oh, yes, they migrate," he was telling her. "I know they migrate."

I loosened my tie. "Well, how's James Joyce coming?"

She held the book up. "This? Well, I don't know. It's certainly very confusing."

"You're so beautiful, Lela."

"Those other books. All you brought me. When am I supposed to have everything read? When do you want me to be through with them?"

"You're so beautiful you make my fingertips buzz."

"I won't get *anything* read at all if you don't give me time to read."

I wear glasses, which is a problem. I like to remove them before I kiss, but to do so gives the whole show away. So without removing my glasses I put my hands on her shoulders and tilted my head, but she saw me coming. She shook her head without moving, her eyes—her lovely pale green eyes—watching me all the while. "No," she said. "Please? No."

I flopped back in the swing and stretched my legs out.

"You have such *long* legs," she said, "and you're so dark. Are you sure you're not half French or something?"

"No, I'm not half French, or something. Listen, Lela, I want to respect you. I want to respect you and like you. I don't *want* to patronize you, but if you insist on going on being so genteel about everything, then . . ."

"Good heavens," she said, surprised. "*Would* you respect me if I were different?"

"If we had an affair, you mean? Is this a fair translation of what you're trying to tell me now? Yes, of course. That's the point. This would be an honest reaction."

"Well, and *I* say that's a very funny way of looking at things. Would you really want me to go around having affairs with every man I met? Really? I don't believe it."

"Oh, God, Lela, I didn't say every man you met. Look. *Do* you want to go on seeing me, or not?"

She shook her head. "No—Yes—No—I don't know. Yes, we'd better stop seeing each other," she said.

"Forever and ever and ever and ever?"

"Yes."

I stood up. "All right, that's it then. At least that's a definite answer."

"Yes," she said, "it's a definite answer."

I left the porch and crossed the lawn without looking back. When I reached my drive, she called, and I was ready to sprint back, but when I turned around she was merely waving. I waved and went into the house, leaving her still standing on the porch. I felt very definitely deflated.

In the morning I decided I had only myself to blame. I had moved too quickly and been too confident. What I needed was the athlete's casual looseness—a change of pace. I had other friends, other contacts.

I started going to some parties, and I spent a lot of spare time hanging around a tiny blonde named Catherine E.

THE MADAME BOVARY COMPLEX

Bavender. I later married her. She was home from Smith for the summer, and she wanted to write. She was working on a novel about adolescent sexual awakening. She wrote a little like Tom Wolfe. This surprised everyone because she was such a small, fragile girl. My mother never really liked her. She thought Catherine was sweet, all right, but she never really went for her. Catherine was a New England girl, and *she* put out the first time we met, which, looking back on it now, was one of the few simple, unequivocal things she ever did. I probably married her on the strength of it.

Meanwhile, Lela was very busy gardening next door. She hauled mulch and chemical sprays around in a red metal wheelbarrow. I would see her in shorts in the backyard, and we would wave. She had the setter loose when Dwight was gone, and the dog didn't seem to run off anymore. It followed her around. I once asked her how her reading was progressing. I was getting ready to go to a party, and I'd come out to get a white shirt off the back line for my mother to iron. "Oh," she said, "pretty good. I'll send some of those books back one of these days." I couldn't see what with all the activity in the backyard how she ever got any reading done.

Then she turned up at the Eddelson party in mid-August. Catherine and I had been playing badminton out in their poorly lighted court, and when my eyes started to bother me, I turned her over to one of the Eddelson boys to finish the game while I went into the house to get a drink. I found Lela sitting on the sunporch with a group of women. They were all mothers except for her, and except for her, they were all talking about Dr. Spock. It is a curious thing how I could have seen her around women like that so often without realizing how much she wanted and needed a child—not art, not books, not music. In any case, I'm trying to say that this moment was a turning point in our relationship because as I passed without even speaking I realized what was essentially so disturbing about everything. I was in love. I loved her. I felt shaken. I felt dizzy, but I went on into the other room to see if there was any gin left.

I asked her later if Dwight was around, and when she said no, I asked her if she wanted a ride home. She said, "Oh, yes, I guess," without much enthusiasm.

It was beginning to rain when we left. We could hear it in the foliage overhead, and when we got into the car I put the windshield wiper on. She sat next to me without speaking, but she filled me with such alarm just by being there that I could hardly wait to get the car away from the Eddelson place. I didn't show it. I kept my old tone from habit: a smooth preoccupation with language first, and nothing—actually nothing—to suggest that the words themselves meant anything.

I knew that she would probably not let me into the house, and I swung along the shore road looking for a place to park, like a teenager, like a desperate high school boy. Lela chose not to notice what we were doing, but when I stopped the car, she said, "Oh, where are—?" But I covered her mouth with mine, my hands working to get

THE MADAME BOVARY COMPLEX

themselves between her back and the car seat. "Oh, this isn't right, this just isn't right," she said several times between kisses. I unbuttoned her blouse, and when she saw her breasts beginning to appear she pulled me up against her with enormous force. By now it was pouring. We sat in our steel shell encased with rain, hugging and moaning.

Then I told her I loved her. She shook her head. She looked startled. She put her hand over my mouth. "No," she said, "you mustn't say that again. Ever."

"Do you love me?"

"I'm going to tell you once—just once. Then I want you to take me home. Yes, I love you. More than the sun, the moon, the stars. Take me home now, Dick."

I fussed and fumed, but I couldn't get anywhere. She wouldn't even argue. I was finally enraged because I was filled with such bitterness. I was a young man. I couldn't understand. "I know what's wrong with you," I finally said. "Nobody's going to pry you loose from the Woolgrove money, are they?"

She put her hand over her eyes, but still said nothing.

When we reached her house, we saw Dwight's car in the garage. "Oh," she said, "he'll be worried. Don't get out. Don't get wet. I'll run up myself."

She was gone before I could protest. I watched the front door close behind her. I thought about Dwight in his floppy shorts and big shoes. Then I broke. I was beside myself.

I got out of the car, and standing on their lawn in the downpour, I yelled. I yelled and yelled. Only the sound of

139

the rain could have kept my voice from carrying to my parents' house next door. "Come back out," I said, "or I'm coming in to get you, Lela. Do you hear me? I'm not going to put up with this any longer! Come out! Come out!"

Dwight thought I was drunk. He came down the walk carrying an umbrella. "Come on in the house, old sport," he said, "come on in. We'll see if we can't get you some black coffee."

I stared at him for a minute, then turned and ran back to the car. I drove back to the Eddelson place, and in my soaked clothes wandered around through the last of the party looking for Catherine, but she had gone home.

When I woke the next morning, the sky was clear. From my bedroom window I could hear the Woolgroves' lawn mower going next door. Dwight was cutting the grass. He liked to do his own yard work. She was sitting on the stoop watching him. They both looked as if nothing—absolutely nothing—had ever happened to them in their whole lives.

When the train pulled into the station, I got my bag down from the overhead rack and threw my overcoat over my arm. Catherine had at last completed *the* definitive novel on adolescent sexual awakening. It was about loneliness, alienation, and longing. She thought she was a pretty big woman now. She believed that, overnight, she was going to become the idol of every adolescent. Adolescents as a rule do not think much about alienation. It is not a common topic of conversation with them. Catherine had gone up to the lake to work on an editor's suggestion for some last-

THE MADAME BOVARY COMPLEX

minute improvements—like trying to find a way to cut a hundred pages. I did not know how I was going to tell my parents about the coming divorce. They were getting old now, and I inflicted on them as few of my own troubles as I could. I believed that it was a woman's job to tell them, but Catherine had never been close to my people.

A somber glow was in the air, and a storm was forming over the railway station. The birds were talking in the parking lot in back. I wondered if Lela still hauled mulch and chemical sprays around in the red wheelbarrow. I saw her in the mind's eye kneeling in the garden behind the house, wearing battered work gloves and cutting the roses back for the winter. I was moved by all those lonely, prayerless souls who wake in the middle of the night to shut the window against the first sharp hoarfrost, knowing that the roses have been trimmed, the mulch put down, the shears stored on their shelf in the garage, beside the rake, the hose, the fertilizers and the power mower which sleeps under its plastic cover the long golden sleep of the just. Then shame and self-hatred suddenly coursed through my whole being, as if filling my veins and tissues, and I suddenly saw myself being pursued and overtaken by every delusion, lie, and vanity which this mysterious universe has to offer.

The
Cage

        I came up to the mountains to get a fresh start, to begin with practically nothing. I rented the abandoned cabin in the middle of nowhere on impulse, a place that hadn't been used for years, but when I'd put the money down and brought my things—the cage standing out there in the back of the closed truck—I already felt faintly disenchanted. The close, unfiltered mountain sun was on my neck and along my arms, but the porch posts smelled damp, and a large blotch of dark spring wet was spread across the porch in front of the door.

        I unlocked the door and stepped inside, just across the sill. I stood there in the silence, breathing the damp air, like enclosed icebox chill. The old lumber nailed across the windows cast areas of darkness which were partly broken by thin, intervening strips of white morning light. Scattered piles of pale, grayish moths lay under the newspaper-covered beds, and some still lived, beating against the uneven folds of the stained curtains their grayish wing dust. Upturned wasps, dried out and perfect, lay along the narrow windowsills beside bluish, big-bottomed flies. General sift was everywhere—on the chairs, the round, bare dining room tabletop, the cold hearth, the faded, mismatched throw-rugs which people take to the mountains rather than toss out.

I had to get some hot water because everything was going to need scrubbing. I couldn't stay in the place another minute without doing something about it. I took the newspapers from the beds and found kindling in the kitchen woodbox. I got everything settled in front of the stove and then very gradually teased the small slivers of wood and crumpled newspaper into ascending energy. I fed on the heavier stuff slowly. Fragile tips cracked, scenting the kitchen. Smoke curled through the rings on the tops of the stove, where the metal plates were set, and I adjusted the damper.

Behind a curtain, in a storage closet, I located two pails, a broom, a mop, a saw, and an ax. I took the pails out and let the curtain fall. I carried the empty pails out of the cabin and onto the screened porch. I had not seen the creek yet, but I could hear it far below, running between the aspen and the heavy mountain brush.

As I walked down the slope in front of the cabin, the sun was hot on my back, but the air, moistened near the creek, was cool and fragrant, and along the creek bank the grass was still holding the morning damp. I bent down in the long, wet grass and one-at-a-time pushed the pails in under, steadying them against the current. When I went back up the steep slope, trying to find my footing among the rocks, my shoulders began to ache, and I set the pails down three times to change my grip.

I got the ax out of the closet, and while I waited for the pails to warm on the stove, I pried the lumber away from the windows. I worked awkwardly and painfully because I had to keep my arms above my head. When I had cleared a window with the side of the cumbersome ax, I pulled out the remaining nails with my fingers, slowly working them loose from the softened, wet wood. The sun rose toward noon, and on my way around the cabin to get to the back, I stopped to take off my shirt. It was strangely satisfying work—as if I were helping the cabin to breathe a little better.

I worked through the lunch hour and on into the late afternoon—cleaning the large central room with the fireplace, the two small, curtained, cell-like bedrooms, and the tiny kitchen with its iron stove, big woodbox and shelves covered with yellow oilcloth. The kitchen also had a sink and workable-looking faucets, as if someone had once seriously considered putting in a pump to get water from the creek below, but aside from the useless sink, there was no plumbing in the house.

I cleaned the outhouse last—a hundred feet or so from the cabin, among some cool, tall firs. I had stayed away from it on purpose because I had been afraid of what it was going to look like. The outhouse had not been used

THE CAGE

for some time, of course, and while it was filled with cobwebs and general dirt, it was not too objectionable. I removed the cobwebs and dumped some strong lye down
there in the dark, but when I was through I came out and
urinated on the grass behind it.

I was finished—through. I was numb with exhaustion
and covered with sweat. I looked at my watch, going back
to the cabin, and found it was a little after six o'clock. I
went into the cabin, straightened the rugs, put the chairs
back in place, made a final test for dust, took one last long
look, and then went on out to the closed truck.

Now: Was I going to have trouble getting the cage out
of the truck and into the cabin? I'd cleaned the cabin with
the cage constantly in the back of my mind without asking
that question before.

The rocky, curving trail in from the road did not go directly up to the cabin, and I had already driven the truck
in as close to the cabin as I could get it. I was going to
have to haul the cage across a hundred feet or so of rough,
open field, and then up the small rise to the front porch. It
was going to be much more awkward than heavy—a big
man on each side could have carried it—but I was going to
have to push and tug and fight with it. I wondered if I was
going to have trouble getting it through the porch door,
then up the porch and angled right for going through the
cabin. I wondered if I were going to have to take the
hinges off the doors. I couldn't remember where I had
packed my tool kit. Everything seemed hopeless . . .

I was suddenly so weary that I thought about leaving the

cage in there overnight and getting a fresh start in the morning. However, I didn't want to face it in the morning, either. I was going to have a big day tomorrow trying to gather wood. I marched up to the truck, opened the back panels and addressed the darkness inside.

"All right, you monster," I said resignedly, "let's get set. Here we go . . ."

I did not start the fire in the home for retarded children. Whatever the world would say when it caught me, I did not start the fire in the home for retarded children. I was simply walking in the woods when the flames shot up. There were two of them together—a pale, slender boy and this girl, perhaps brother and sister—but when I went closer to comfort them, the boy turned and fled. While he ran, he kept looking back over his shoulder. Well, I was going to have enough trouble with one. She stood there, staring, her face black with soot, her dress torn at the shoulders and at the seams around the bare knees.

"Everything's going to be all right," I kept saying, in a soft, soothing voice. "Oh yes, everything's going to be all right."

She half reclines in the corner of the cage with legs curled under her, watching. She has her long, flat hair down to one side of her face, and when I come near, just to shove the food through the bars, she pulls her head back abruptly, redistributing the hair. She seldom speaks these days, and I am afraid she is slowly becoming more animal-like than not. I have ceaselessly fought this by having the two of us as a team embark on a program in the Great

Books. I will bring over to the cage when the day's work is done something from Aeschylus or Plato, and during these long evenings together by the cabin fire, I will sometimes read the same passages over and over aloud.

I will read these things in English, not in Greek—she doesn't, of course, know Greek—and I will stop from time to time to explain the difficult parts. We also study the great religions of the world and try to decide what religion we would choose if we could go to church—if we could get the cage into a church, which we can't. I will never know what she comprehends and doesn't. However—and this is the important thing—I will never, never give up. I suppose I was born to teach.

I had a constant problem in the mountains with wood. The wood-gathering became the thread of my existence, the center of my thoughts. We needed a fire in the middle of August, an hour after the sun went down, and when the leaves turned all around us, I could imagine what the winter up there was going to be like. I could never get in enough wood to take care of more than one extra night, in case of wet weather, but with the winter coming on, and snow on the ground, I was going to need a heavy reserve, brought down and stored on the front porch.

I went out to look for wood every morning after breakfast, while the coolness still lingered, and I was fresh. I walked until I came to the clearing—my clearing now— filled with fallen timber and stumps. I did not know wood, and at first I could not begin to guess what was going to burn and what was not. I sometimes found stumps that roared for hours on their own pitch, as if soaked in fuel, but when I dragged back the next day what looked to be the same stuff, I wouldn't have the same luck.

I chopped in the clearing to get the stumps into some manageable shape, and when I had a good-sized load, I dragged them back through the twisting forest path two-at-a-time, around the trees, fighting to avoid the snags. With pounding heart, and having trouble breathing, I would have to stop every few feet, and, by midday, when the clearing was filled with heat and light like a beach, I could no longer manipulate my sore fingers inside the stiff gloves.

I sometimes vary our reading programs with a little music. I play cello. I set the music stand up in front of the cage, drag a chair over, and begin. She sits quietly, curious, wondering, her head to one side, listening—but soon she's scratching herself again. "A bath for you, I think soon," I say, but go on with the cello for the time being. I move the chair a little further away from the cage.

But always the problem about wood! I finally realized that I could not possibly get in enough to last us through the winter months, when, in all likelihood, drifts could keep us inside for weeks at a time, possibly months. I was going to have to appeal to the outside.

I went to town and ordered some, and when the truck came out several days later, I set up the cello beside the cage and began to play, hoping to cover any little noises she made. I played on and on while the man prowled around outside the cabin for an hour, emptying the truck, piling, and stacking. Oh, he was slow, neat, methodical! I got so stiff in that one position!

I finally laid down the instrument and took the check out to him—a big boy with close-cropped reddish hair and fair, freckled skin. He was smoking a cigar. He wiped his big palm off on the side of his pants before touching the check. She made a little noise inside, just then, but I was looking him directly in the eyes at the time, and I saw no change of expression. I went back inside and picked up the cello.

I was in the woods behind the cabin a few days later when I saw him again. He was wearing a hunting jacket and carrying a gun under his arm, loosely, casually pointed at the ground, in professional fashion. He was smoking his cigar. I asked him if he would mind not hunting on my land. I told him I was against all forms of killing. He tipped his cap at me and disappeared.

I had both stillness and racket to master. I soon became the stillness in the mountains, in the levels of pines in the uneven clearing. I moved garbed in brilliant stillness through the days, in complexly orchestrated quiet, but the nights were another matter—never completely solved.

In the nights the rushing creek below entered the stillness and disintegrated it. The water's noise was now magnified, as if the creek had become a cascading torrent just outside the cabin. I began to imagine that my friend was stalking out there, carrying his gun, munching his cigar, getting nearer and nearer, ready to try the door. I slept uneasily under the waterfall of sounds and lost voices, but when I stirred in the morning, in the first, faint, chilly light, I woke in time to hear the creek quieting and retreating. Oh, there is nothing more peaceful—more close to the Creator—than a pure mountain morning!

Ah!

But who bears more of bliss than just the seeming so!

I was watching her bathe when I saw him again. I was sitting on the creek bank in the tall grass, holding her leash in my hands, and thinking about—what? Nothing. Possibly about how happy I was. I was.

The sun filled the heavy brush around the creek with dense warmth. Small circles of insects hovered over the current, and the early afternoon air was resonant with insect sounds. Birds called, out of sight. Then everything— in a moment, in a split second—was gone, like a dream.

He was just a glimpse—just a hunting cap—on the other side, back in the bush. I stood up slowly, my heart pounding, and keeping my voice steady, I called her. I called out once, holding the towel. I dared not look across the creek again. She came up on all fours, getting a grip on the grass above the bank with both hands. When she stood up and I looked into her eyes, I could see that she had already sensed something. She followed me up to the cabin drying her hair on the way.

Everything is altered by that much. We stay inside the cabin inside our shrinking Eden. I do not go out except to get water from the stream or grab some wood from the front porch, quickly slamming the door behind me. I feel, in that moment when I turn my back, that someone is watching. I can not sleep. I seldom leave the cage. Reading

THE CAGE

helps. I read aloud, much of the night, or play cello. We are reading *The Decline and Fall of the Roman Empire* together, for the prose. She sometimes makes little restless sounds in her cage. She seems possessed by tension. She sometimes reminds me of a coiled spring. Is she waiting? Or do I imagine it? I worry about her. I let the house go. The general sift returns . . .

I wake one night in my chair. The fire is slowly going out. The fall winds moan. She is sleeping. I see a face at the window. I can just make out the round whiteness, not see concrete features. He is himself no more than a dream, a shadow. Yes. I have fully decided this—a dream. We are safe. We are civilized beings who inhabit a classic world of order and calm.

Then he moves. The fleshy upper lip is turned slightly, showing big white teeth. He grins.

All right, I think, let's have it out, then, once and for all, man-to-man. I creep through the kitchen, open the back door, get in my truck, and try to run him down. I race up the pitched incline after him—around and around and around. I finally get him. I lug him up into the woods behind the outhouse.

When I come back to the cabin, my chest is heaving. She is awake. She is making her noises again. She holds her hands clasped behind her neck and sways her upper torso, moaning. I play the cello for awhile, hoping to calm her, but she is hardly listening.

I could not have anticipated what the winter would be like

up there alone. The drifts sealed us in. The drifts and the silence. The creek froze—stilling the lost voices and the last of everything. Yes, the last of everything. In the nights the animals moving down from the high places paused to sniff at the cabin, but went on. In the nights I imagined *he* came back from time to time to look around, to try the doors, but I could not sustain this image for long. I would wake up, thinking he was at the door, but it would be no more than the winds, sometimes less than the wind. His absence was the final silence, the complete vacuum . . .

I fall into uneasy dreams—dreams more real than the face at the window.

Sometimes the cage is standing open, everybody gone. I can see the empty cage, the empty rooms, as if I am looking down at a doll's house with no roof. The fire is still burning, the bed needs making, the cello rests on a chair, a window is half raised, and the curtain blows in . . .

Sometimes he comes back. We three are crashing around the room together, upsetting the furniture, throwing things. We three are engaged in awful violence, but the whole process is vaguely automatic and joyful, as if we were three children indulging in a bedtime game . . .

Sometimes he is in the cage with her. This is the worst. They are living together in there. They make no effort to take care of the cage or themselves, and everything soon becomes impossibly filthy. They eat whatever I throw them. They lie around. They have absolutely no shame. They copulate in front of me, like beasts, from behind. I take up the cello, my back to them, and try playing . . .

THE CAGE

Oh, Lord, that winter! Blackness! There were no stars, no moon. Blackness? Even the mountains disappeared. We suffered the silence together—a silence which was so general and so profound the cello's small cry sounded like the last, faint screech of moral indignation and human pain . . .

I *need* him. Where is he? I sometimes forget. Then, at other times, I see the body in my mind's eye, out there behind the outhouse, which, in actuality, must be by now covered with snow, drifts of ice and snow.

I wonder, at times, in moments of irrationality, if he weren't the lost brother—the youth who had fled at the sight of me years ago, in the other woods, because, if so, then *he* is Adam. And I am . . .

O isolated being! How can I go on?

When—how, where, at what point—did everything change? When I took her out of the cage one morning to sponge her down . . .

(She doesn't want to go back in. I let her play on the floor beside the fire. Where is the harm? I can pretend for awhile that she is someone. When I start the breakfast she wants to help. So sweet . . . I let her try setting the table. I am surprised with the results. I let her try setting *two* places. I find out that eating with her isn't an overwhelming success, but I decide to try other things. We dress her up—a gown I found on the closet floor, some heels, a hat, and we comb her hair. She finds the lipstick herself. She smears her mouth horribly, like a large crack in a doll's face, but I do not interfere. She flops around a bit, in the heels, but she is very proud. She stands in front of the mirror, turning this way and that, testing. She doesn't want to go back into the cage . . .

You should see the two of us sitting across from each other at that huge round, rough wood dining room table—alone in the vast winter night—her food going on both sides of her plate onto the floor. She has taken off her shoes for comfort, while she is eating, and they have been very carefully placed, one on each side of her plate, within casual reach . . .

I rattle the bars. I rattle the bars when she gets up in the morning. I rattle the bars through the day. I get nowhere. When she goes into the kitchen, or steps onto the front porch, I can not see her from the cage, and I worry. She has learned to use matches . . .

She likes the cello. She sits down, wearing her hat and gown, picks the instrument up and begins, imitating the way I hold it. I have at least taught her something. She almost looks intelligent in that position, in the chair beside the cage.

She is pregnant. What can I do about it? How can I tell her? What does she know? What will happen? She is *pregnant*.

She likes the cello. She sits down to play, all dressed up. She makes a hideous racket with it, absolutely appalling. I put my hand over my ears, but I can not drown out the sound. Her idea of music goes on and on and on . . .

THE CAGE